www.ChloeEmile.com

Bon Appétit, Chérie

A French Kiss Romantic Comedy

CHLOE EMILE

This is a work of fiction. Names, characters, organizations, places, events, and incidents are either products of the author's imagination or are used fictitiously. Some locations in Paris are real, and others are fictitious.

ISBN-13: 978-1987859188
ISBN-10: 1987859189

CONTENTS

CHAPTER ONE

"*I*t's game day!" Philippe rubbed his hands together as he stood in his kitchen on set of the wildly popular cooking show, *Ultimate Food Fighter*. He watched the show's host get ready to take her spot in front of the camera to kick off the segment, and he scoped out the judges' table. He couldn't help but smile at them, especially the beautiful tall judge whose nametag read "Gianna."

She smiled back at him.

"Welcome to *Ultimate Food Fighter*! Today we are coming to you live from Los Angeles, California," the host said to the camera. "Here on the show, three chefs compete head-to-head in a two-round, grueling competition in the place they know best: the kitchen. If you're just tuning in, the rules are simple. Contestants are given one main ingredient for each round. Their job is to cook a dish highlighting that ingredient, and our judges will then give one chef the title of Ultimate Food Fighter, along with a grand prize of ten thousand euros. Today, we have an incredible line-up of three chefs from around Europe. Our first contestant is Adolfo Donati from Fiesole, Italy."

The camera zoomed over to Adolfo's kitchen, and he waved as the crowd cheered.

"Our second contestant is Katrin Zetterberg of Stockholm, Sweden."

The camera turned its attention to Katrin, and she smiled widely at the lens and the crowd.

"Finally, our third contestant is Philippe Deneuve of Paris, France. Let's give all of our contestants a warm welcome."

On cue, the audience roared with applause, whooping and hollering.

"Contestants, are you ready? On the count of three, start your cooking! One, two, THREE!"

The timer set for thirty minutes appeared on a giant screen. Philippe, along with the other contestants, raced to unveil the secret ingredient of the first round. The ingredient sat under a silver, domed tray, and Philippe lifted the dome and saw what they had to work with the freshwater fish, pike.

Philippe knew exactly what to do as the perfect dish popped into his mind. *Pochouse.* On his way to the communal ingredients, he noticed that Katrin had her A-game face on. Adolfo, on the other hand, looked as though he wasn't quite sure how to attack his dish just yet.

Philippe opened the fridge and scanned it for eel. No such luck. *That's okay, I can sub bacon for eel.* He took out a package of thick-cut pork, along with a pack of butter. He grabbed the other ingredients he needed and, with his arms full, raced back to his counter space.

As the first chef to have all his ingredients back at his workstation, Philippe threw his hands up to generate a cheer from the audience. One of his favorite parts about cooking in front of a crowd was inviting them into his world, into his kitchen.

He got right to work, blanching the bacon. While the water boiled, he chopped the carrots and celery but not without wowing the crowd by chopping the veggies into perfect, uniform-sized morsels in record time. He juggled the spice jars of salt, pepper, and cayenne before adding dashes to the pot of broth. He deboned the fish and reveled in the "oohs" and "ahhs" coming from the bleachers of fans. As he multitasked, he willed himself to stay traditional, especially with this classic recipe from the fishermen of Burgundy.

At twenty-five, Philippe was a baby in the food industry, yet he had plenty of drive and ambition to make it to the top. He had graduated first in his class from a top-tier, prestigious culinary institute in the heart of Paris, and he had earned a sous-chef position in a five-star restaurant right out of school. He attributed much of his drive to his family. As one of the middle children in the large Deneuve family, he'd often felt overshadowed by his brothers and sisters. He wasn't the strong muscle man like Xavier. He wasn't the musically gifted one like Mathieu. Yet he had a knack for cooking and decided at an early age that he wanted to be a chef. It was his heart's work.

In culinary school, he had a taste of what it felt like to shine. He rocked the kitchen, repeatedly receiving compliments from the tough instructors of his garde manger classes, and baked with exquisite precision. For the first time, he felt as though he was good at something, and he wanted more and more of it. Philippe constantly pushed himself to be not only a better chef but the best chef.

That sometimes meant he was a little crazy and outlandish with his creations. His mentor and boss, Arnauld Beauchene, had said that that could make Philippe's work too unapproachable and had urged him over and over to blend contemporary with the traditional, which was why Philippe was going for the pochouse today.

He looked at the clock and saw that he had two minutes left—just enough time to plate the stew and make it look appetizing. By itself, pochouse wasn't overly impressive. Philippe garnished three bowls with fresh parsley, then placed each bowl on a large, white square plate and added a stylish row of a beet and butter sauce for color.

The show's host called time just as he finished the last plate's presentation. His creation was whisked away to the judge's table, and just like that, it was time for round two: the main course. He tried not to think about the judges deliberating over his first course and focused his attention on the domed platter hiding ingredient number two.

The show's host rambled in the background, pumping up and entertaining the crowd. During the commercial breaks, seats were called at random, and the person in that seat got the opportunity to try exotic foods like merguez, sausage in a lamb intestine casing, or fufu, a bread made with cassava flour in Ghana. Since they were filming in the United States, they also focused on some of the local culinary scene.

After the dishes were presented, all eyes were on the judges. In *Ultimate Food Fighter*, one chef was kicked out of the kitchen after the first challenge was completed. Who would it be? Philippe wanted to know but hid any insecurity behind a confident façade as the judges tried the round-one dishes. First up was Katrin's dish: lutfisk, a fish-and-potatoes dish. The judges tasted and deliberated.

Judge #2, Marc, was also Parisian. He chewed longer than the average person would have and swallowed. "It's a little overcooked, but the flavor is there."

Katrin's dish was ranked 8.5 out of 10, which was a fine score.

Adolfo's dish was next on the chopping block. Like Philippe, he had also made a soup, but Adolfo's had a tomato base—a tomato-infused broth with roasted cherry tomatoes sitting atop the white broiled fish.

Philippe saw it in the judges' faces as they each slurped a spoonful of the red soup: much too acidic. He was right. Adolfo's score was a 6.

Philippe was feeling hopeful. The audience watched with hawk-like eyes, waiting to see which contestant would snag the win. He watched Gianna take a little test bite.

"I don't like fish, but this is good!" she said.

The crowd cheered, and Philippe relaxed.

The other two judges weren't as impressed. The French judge claimed the fish was rubbery, and the third judge, a food critic, said that the dish needed a little more salt. Philippe's heart sank.

The judges deliberated for a moment before announcing Philippe's score.

Gianna was the one to say, "Philippe Deneuve, 8 stars out of 10! Round two will be a dueling battle between Katrin and Philippe."

Philippe would have preferred first place—who wouldn't have?—but second place would at least take him into round two. That was all that mattered right now.

"All right, contestants!" the host called. "Let's see what your next dishes will be made of... one, two, THREE!"

Under the dome lay a rich, beautiful cut of beef. Philippe had an idea for his recipe, but it might be a risk because of time. Philippe scratched his head and saw Katrin head to the communal ingredients. Maybe she wasn't the weakest link in the competition after all, as he'd originally thought.

"Oh, what the heck," Philippe muttered and made his way over to find the ingredients for *boeuf a la bourguignonne*. He could make that dish blindfolded, but the question was: could he make a grand-prize winner in under two hours? Philippe was about to find out.

Katrin was already chopping onions. Philippe knew he had to tune out the competition. The ingredient list for *boeuf a la bourguignonne* was long, but fortunately, the communal pantry had everything he needed, down to the cognac and Cote du Rhone. Getting back into the groove, he cubed the chuck meat and seared it in hot oil. The minutes ticked by as the meat and vegetables simmered. Lost in his art, he added tomato paste and thyme and sautéed mushrooms.

While the beef simmered, he had just enough time to grab a baguette and make a simple garlic bread to serve alongside his main dish. He tried a taste of his *boeuf a la bourguignonne* and kissed his fingertips. The audience applauded, knowing that his dish was a success! With two minutes left on the timer, he hastily arranged his creation until it looked as if a food photographer had styled it. *Perfect!*

The audience counted down to the final second. "Three! Two! One!"

"Time!" the show's host called out, and he, along with Katrin, threw his hands in the air. "Now it's time for the judges to taste our round-two dishes and find out who will be named the Ultimate Food Fighter."

Philippe watched as his *boeuf a la bourguignonne* was whisked over to the judges' table. Two of the judges seemed to fade away into the background, the pretty brunette standing out among them. Gianna.

The host, talking right at the audience, said, "All right! Congrats, competitors!"

It didn't matter how many times he competed in cooking competitions or how many times a customer tried his food. That first taste was always nerve-racking. Would they love it? Spit it out? Tell their friends to never try his restaurant? Would the critic give him a bad review and publish it in a magazine for everyone to see?

Once again, the judges tried their dishes. Philippe's was first, but he felt confident in his rich beef dish. He watched as each of the judges took a bite off of the plate.

"The presentation is phenomenal," the food critic judge said, taking a second bite. More than one bite was a good sign.

Gianna smiled. "There's nothing negative to say."

The others nodded. Philippe got a 10 out of 10. A perfect score!

The judges moved to Katrin's dish, a beef stew called kalops. The judges tasted and deliberated. Parisian chef Marc commented that the dish was wonderful but not overly complex in flavor. Her final score was an 8.5, making Philippe the grand winner.

The host presented Philippe with a check and a cheesy trophy featuring a knife block. He waved at the crowd, shook hands with Katrin, and enjoyed the moment of success that he could add to his resume. He had officially joined the circle of Ultimate Food Fighters.

CHAPTER TWO

One bite of Philippe Deneuve's cooking made the top American model realize that she wanted Philippe Deneuve—for his cooking, of course. She was in the process of opening up a restaurant, and she hadn't yet found the perfect chef.

Gianna Delano was determined to have a business chat with Philippe, but he had to fly back to France immediately after thc episode finished filming. Fortunately, it took just a short conversation with the show's producer to find out more about him.

Philippe was a chef at the five-star restaurant, *Maison de Beauchene*, in the heart of Paris. After she changed out of her studio outfit, she left to battle the atrocious LA traffic.

She wanted to check on the construction progress at her restaurant. She entered the building through the back entrance, also known as the future employee entrance and trash drop-off area. She looked around and marveled that the space was coming alive with her vision. *Chic, Mais Oui!* was her baby, her contemporary French-inspired concept.

She would serve French fare with unusual twists. She wanted to blend the traditional and the new. Buckwheat crepes filled with modern, funky combinations. Baked Camembert meets Southern-style American biscuits. A lamb gigot with trendy grains like quinoa instead of potatoes. Gianna just needed the perfect chef. She had interviewed dozens of hopeful chefs, but no one wowed Gianna, and one thing she had learned was to never, ever settle. Gianna's decisions were always either a resounding yes or an absolute no. As she ran her hands along the walls that still need to be painted, she felt a renewed vigor to find the right chef.

"You're running out of time, Gianna," she said while wiping some sawdust off the countertops.

She did a quick calculation in her mind and realized that she had mere months to find the perfect chef to tie her vision together. But she was positive that Philippe Deneuve was the one who could take her restaurant to the top. She wanted him beside her for the grand opening. She could see them now, standing side by side...

So she did what any sane person would do and bought a ticket for a flight leaving LAX next week. Paris or bust! She must try to lure Philippe to not only become her head chef but to move across the Atlantic Ocean.

***

Gianna opened her eyes and jerked her head at the sound of the flight attendant's voice.

"Ladies and gentlemen, welcome to Paris, France, and the Charles de Gaulle Airport. It is 4:57 p.m. local time, and the temperature is seventy-two degrees. On behalf of American Airlines and the entire crew, I would like to thank you for joining us on this trip. Have a nice day."

The plane was already about halfway through the final descent, which gave Gianna just enough time to wake up from her deep sleep in first class, which was always quieter than business or coach.

She'd been to Paris many times in her modeling career, but she couldn't really believe that she had flown there today for something that might not even happen. *This is crazy.* Yet her intuition had told her to go, so she listened. Gianna recognized that she had only about a three percent chance of succeeding, but as the plane hit the runway with just a little bump, she couldn't help enjoying the thrill of the chase.

By the time she could make it to the address listed on Maison de Bauchene's website, it would already be dinnertime, so trying to talk to him that evening would be impossible. So Gianna took a cab to take her to the Four Seasons.

She opened the door to the taxi and slid her small suitcase on the seat beside her. After years of traveling, she was a carry-on girl for life. Checked bags were overrated–she'd lost one too many suitcases to count–and she always knew what to pack and what to do without.

The driver didn't even bother to turn around. "Où?"

"31 Avenue George V, *s'il vous plait*," she answered.

When Gianna spoke French, she could hear how strong her American accent was. She couldn't roll her R's properly, despite her many attempts, but French people always seemed to think it was cute. Perhaps they were also flattered when foreigners attempted to speak their language, which they naturally assumed was the best language in the world.

Although this would only be a short trip, she loved that her hotel was right off of Champs-Elysees and a smorgasbord of attractions were within walking distance. Avenue Montaigne was one of Gianna's favorite shopping streets, and she was hoping to spend an afternoon at her beloved Jardin des Tuileries. But tonight, Gianna would order room service and sleep off her jet lag. Why was hotel sleep always the best kind of sleep? Gianna yawned at the thought.

The driver pulled up to the front of the hotel, and she paid him. Once she stepped out of the car, she waltzed into the hotel lobby and checked in. Next order of business: food and sleep. Basic human needs with a side of luxury, just as she liked it.

In the late morning, Gianna was ready for her mission—after ordering breakfast to have on her terrace, of course. A café crème with a fresh croissant was all she needed to start her Parisian day. As she dressed in a black sheath dress and simple black heels, she felt as if she was getting ready for a covert spy mission. Her nerves were jangled as if she was taking on an international mystery, not suggesting a slightly preposterous job offer to a very handsome chef. What was the worst possible scenario? He said no. A quick trip to Paris was a side benefit.

She checked the hours of the restaurant on her smartphone and realized that the restaurant would open at eleven thirty for lunch.

Since she was still jetlagged, she lounged around, watching French TV. News, news, and more news. She kept clicking. French TV had a lot of coverage on politics. They often held round-table discussions on serious issues. Her French was good enough that she could follow at least half of what they were saying, but she wanted to watch something that would relax her. Finally she found an old episode of *Friends* dubbed in French and left it on as background noise.

The croissant must've not been so filling, because her stomach was growling two hours later. She went down to a café to grab a quick lunch, a *nicoise salade*, healthy enough to counterbalance her buttery breakfast.

Gianna figured that after the lunch rush was over, the staff at Maison de Beauchene probably had some downtime. She didn't have an appointment or reservation but chose to float into the restaurant to surprise him.

Maison de Beauchene was within walking distance of her hotel. She was a bit nervous, but surely Philippe would recognize her. After all, she had played an integral role in crowning him the Ultimate Food Fighter. He should be thanking her! At least that was what she told herself to pump up her confidence.

She opened one of the double wood doors leading to the restaurant's lobby, and just as she suspected, the place was quiet. Perfect! No chef, owner, or manager ever wanted to be bothered by non-food issues during their peak times.

"Welcome to Maison de Beauchene," a shapely woman greeted her upon entrance.

Gianna instantly noticed that the hostess's outfit was, well, not quite right. Maybe it was the fact that she was wearing brown leggings with a black dress. The dress didn't fit right, but it looked as if she was going for a sophisticated look. The thing was, the woman was pretty. She had curves, gorgeous brown eyes, and impeccable skin that rivaled porcelain dolls. If she didn't have such an upturned nose and piquant lips, she *could've* been a China doll.

"Just one for lunch?" the hostess asked.

Gianna stopped overanalyzing the girl, a habit picked up through her modeling career. Sometimes she felt like a model scout. She wasn't judging, just observing. It looked as if the hostess was doing the same thing to her, but she was definitely judging. Gianna wondered whether that was a definite sneer on her face.

"Oh, no thanks. I'm actually here to see Philippe Deneuve."

"He's not here." The girl put down the menu. "What's your business?"

She had that Parisian... bluntness that Gianna sometimes ran across. It was something she could never quite get used to, and she'd worked in the modeling industry.

"I'm Gianna Delano, and—"

"Why are you here if not to eat?"

"Er, well, I'm getting ready to open my own restaurant in Los Angeles—Chic, Mais Oui!—" Gianna stopped, fearing she'd said too much. She waited expectantly for the girl to say something.

Nothing. This was awkward.

"Are you the hostess?"

The girl looked incredibly irritated by her assumption, giving Giana the evil eye. "No, I'm a *chef*. Penelope Solomon."

Gianna extended her hand, but Penelope didn't take it. Strike two! Wanting to get away from the awful woman as quickly as possible, Gianna asked her again, "Is Philippe around?"

Penelope didn't answer. Instead, she motioned for Gianna to sit at a table in the nearly empty dining room. Gianna obliged, although a simple yes or no would have been sufficient.

"What business do you have talking to Philippe, a chef at our restaurant?" Penelope asked as she sat across from her.

Gianna was just thankful that Penelope didn't sit beside her.

"Actually, I was a guest judge on a TV show, *Ultimate Food Fighter*," Gianna said. "Philippe and I were on the same episode, and I wanted to talk to him."

Penelope raised her eyebrows. "You were a judge? For a food competition? Honey, it looks like you don't even eat."

Strike three! Gianna hated when people told her she needed to eat a cheeseburger or made other insensitive comments on her weight. People usually assumed that because she was skinny and a model, she had an eating disorder. That was an especially common assumption in the modeling world. Sure, she had known many models with disordered eating patterns. She also knew many who worked hard, atc well, and had good genes. She fell into the latter category.

Modeling might've been a serious career option for those who had won the genetic lottery, but Gianna viewed the opportunity as a stepping stone. She was blessed to have made enough money from modeling part time to fund her education. After she got her business degree, she modeled full time, and she got to travel around the world to work with creative people. Now she had enough savings to pursue her dream of opening a restaurant, and she didn't want it to be the only one either.

But being a model wasn't the easy ride that people assumed it was. It was competitive, and there was plenty of rejection. Clients would tell her to her face what was wrong with her: her legs were too skinny, her boobs weren't big enough, her boobs were too big, she needed to go blond, she needed a nose job, just a little one, etc. In her early twenties, she became immune to their criticisms because she realized it was all nonsense. She would never be perfect, but she was fine the way she was. If clients didn't like her, they shouldn't hire her. The funny thing was, when she stopped caring so much about what other people thought, she got more and more modeling work.

Although she wasn't a supermodel—the way Giselle, Kate Moss, or Naomi Campbell were—she worked regularly and had established herself enough to invited to appear on small cable cooking shows like *Ultimate Food Fighter*. People recognized her from high-profile campaigns. Sometimes she drove strangers crazy because they couldn't place where they'd seen her.

She was a hard worker, but since her industry was based so much on appearances, hard work alone wouldn't take her to the top. It was all about the looks—whatever kind of look was in at the moment—and luck. Those were both things she couldn't control.

Gianna was fine with being a middle-tier model. What she wanted now was a career that didn't rely on her looks and to use her talents to create her own luck.

But she didn't tell Penelope all that. She decided to stick to business, ignoring Penelope's little jab. There was no reason to poke this beast.

When Gianna didn't reply right away, Penelope made a guess about why Gianna was really there. "You want Philippe to come work for you in Los Angeles, don't you? It's not going to happen."

The blunt way Penelope said it was like a slap in the face.

"I wanted to see if it was even a remote possibility." Gianna wasn't sure if she had made a giant mistake by admitting that to Penelope, but she couldn't retract or erase her comment. She was curious to see how this high-strung, erratic crazy person would react. "His food is remarkable, and I think he would be a perfect fit."

"Ha! I knew it. There's just one problem. Philippe already has a good job. He's a well-paid sous-chef to Arnauld Beauchene. Arnauld is world-renowned. Plus, Philippe's close with his family, who lives in Montmartre. He's got a bunch of brothers and sisters, and cool parents. His life is in France, not the United States of America. And your restaurant, what did you say it was called—Chic, Mais *Non*?"

Gianna certainly didn't want to add any fuel to Penelope's fiery personality, but she did correct her. "Chic, Mais Oui!"

"Sorry." Penelope smirked at Gianna. Yes, Gianna was absolutely certain she was smirking now. "The French food scene is so much more refined here. Why would he want to go cook in the land of fast food and obesity?"

Gianna continued to ignore Penelope's jabs. "If you don't mind me asking, where are you in the chef chain-of-command here?"

"I'm the second sous-chef. Arnauld is head chef. Philippe is the primary sous-chef."

That made more sense. But if Philippe came to Chic, Mais Oui! that would give this girl a clear path to being the primary sous-chef. Couldn't she see that?

"Listen, most start-up restaurants fail," Penelope continued. "I think the statistic is what, twenty-three percent of all new restaurants fail within the first year? There's no way any quality chef would take that chance with an unknown backer."

Gianna knew the statistics. She wasn't going into this operation blindly. She had done her research and had a solid business plan. The LA foodie scene was thriving, and thanks to her modeling career and the fact that her dad was a well-known inventor, she had some celebrity status. Ambition ran through her veins, and she would do everything in her power to make the restaurant a success.

With as much of a condescending tone as possible, Penelope said, "Sweetie, I think that Philippe would absolutely not be interested in your little proposition. He's a real chef, not the Ken to your Barbie."

Gianna was a big enough person to admit that Penelope might be right, but she wouldn't give that woman any satisfaction of knowing that, so she kept her mouth shut.

Penelope stood, indicating that their conversation was done.

"Thanks for your time," Gianna said politely. "Just in case Philippe wants to talk, I'm going to give you my number. I'm staying at the Four Seasons for a few days. I hope you'll pass this along." She opened her clutch purse and handed a business card to Penelope.

Surprisingly, Penelope took it. The real question was, would she give it to him?

"Sure." Penelope walked Gianna to the door. "Be sure to stop in for dinner sometime. You can see what comes out of a real chef's kitchen. *Au revoir!*"

Gianna gave her a friendly wave and stepped outside onto the sunny streets of Paris. She was used to dealing with arrogant people but found the best approach was to remain kind. If you couldn't beat them, rise above them.

She had no idea whether Penelope would give Philippe her card or not. Was that sous-chef simply rude to everyone, or did she think Gianna was competition?

Growing up, Gianna hadn't had the easiest time making female friends. In middle school, a group of girls decided to exclude her and bully her to the point that she had to eat lunch in a bathroom stall. They spread rumors about her and called her stupid... she didn't like to remember that time in her life.

As she got older, she realized that other girls' insecurities didn't reflect on who Gianna was as a person. Like it or not, Gianna was objectively beautiful. She couldn't change herself—not her looks and not her personality—just to be accepted by her peers. Instead, she chose friends who were confident and comfortable in their own skin, who didn't resent the fact that she was a model.

It was still a little disheartening when she encountered someone like Penelope. Why couldn't women build one another up instead of tearing one another down? There was enough beauty to go around. The world would be a much nicer place to live in.

She couldn't let Penelope ruin her plans on this trip. With great determination, Gianna whispered, "I'll be back, Maison de Beauchene."

It looked as though she'd be in Paris for longer than expected. Now that she knew Philippe's family was so close, a new idea was born.

Hello, Paris!

Maybe? Perhaps?

CHAPTER THREE

"*A*rnauld, with spring around the corner, I've created a seasonal menu featuring fresh, lighter entrees, salads, and desserts. I even came up with a new signature drink featuring champagne, whiskey, grenadine, and lime. We can call it the Beauchene. How does that sound?"

Before his boss could interject, Philippe handed him a bar glass with the peach-colored concoction, complete with a fresh pitted cherry and lime and orange slices for garnish.

Arnauld took the glass and sniffed the beverage before taking a sip. "It's a fine flavor but much too girly to have my name on it." He handed the drink back to Philippe. "Besides, you know my stance. The answer is *no*. It doesn't matter how many times you try to persuade me."

Philippe leaned on the immaculately clean stainless steel counter. "Maison de Beauchene has used practically the same menu for the last fifty years. I really think it would be beneficial to add more modern cuisine to our repertoire. Don't you want to even look at what I created?"

"I'll look, but the answer is going to be a big fat no." Arnauld took the thick piece of paper the menu was printed on and read the carefully written descriptions for curried cod and mussels and hazelnut, Nutella, and caramel ice cream sandwiches. "These look good, and you know I think you're a cooking genius. If you weren't, you wouldn't be in my kitchen." Philippe nodded, but Arnauld handed the menu right back. "Our patrons expect a certain quality in their dining experience. Not only that, but they're loyal for the familiarity of the experience."

"Not even the desserts? Can't I add just one or two things? People would go crazy for hazelnut, Nutella, and caramel ice cream sandwiches. I promise if you showed our patrons the dessert tray with something like that, they would get dessert just to try it, even if they were so stuffed they wished they could unbutton their pants."

Arnauld laughed but still disagreed with Philippe.

Determined to get one of his creations onto the menu, Philippe tried to negotiate some of his more traditional items. "What about the eggplant and feta gateau with tomato relish? We could create a menu insert and just see how guests respond to some of this."

For a moment, Arnauld considered it. "Nope."

"Not even the risotto Nero with fried octopus and pesto dressing?" Philippe raised his eyebrows. He thought the menu desperately needed a sprucing, a spring cleaning of sorts.

"You know the answer."

Philippe swallowed his disappointment. He flashed Arnauld one of his devastatingly handsome half-smiles. Even when Philippe was upset, he smiled. "I'll keep this around, just in case you decide to change your mind."

"Look, there's no denying these items are fantastic. They just aren't the right fit for my kitchen," Arnauld said. "I'm such a stickler about this because my menu isn't broken. It works. There's nothing to fix. Now, we have a big engagement party in the back room tonight, so get to it! Chop, chop!"

Later that evening, Philippe worked alongside Penelope. He vigorously chopped onions and carrots and celery, the *mirepoix* for many things in the kitchen. Normally, he did even the most menial tasks with his upbeat charm, but tonight, he was too upset over Arnauld's rejection to do more than his job.

"Whoa, what did the onion do to you?" Penelope straightened her white chef's hat with her elbow then went back to sautéing the spinach over the open flame of the giant gas-fired stovetop.

"I'm fine," he replied curtly.

"Fine? That's what a girl says when something is clearly not okay. Talk to me."

As he chopped, Philippe bitterly told Penelope all about his conversation with Arnauld earlier, keeping his voice down so that his boss didn't hear him. Although, he was so angry that he didn't really care if Mr. Beauchene heard exactly what he had to say! He talked and chopped and talked and chopped much more than he needed to, but he found a release in chopping vegetables into perfectly uniform pieces. Cooking was his outlet, his form of expression.

"It's just, Penelope, I feel like he is holding back all of my culinary creativity. It's stifling. Like being trapped in a coffin with no way out."

Penelope added more olive oil to her pan before throwing more handfuls of baby spinach in the cast-iron skillet. Tonight's special was foie gras with garlic spinach and Boursin cheese scalloped potatoes. With as much spinach as she was sautéing, each plate would hold more greens than duck.

Penelope also figured this might've been the correct time to tell Philippe about the visitor from earlier, although for some reason, she didn't really want to. She wanted to withhold this information and let it wilt and writher like the spinach she was cooking. Seeing Philippe's frustration, she felt bad for him.

Playing innocent, Penelope said, "That reminds me, someone came in the restaurant earlier. She was looking for you. Her name was Brianna or Gianna, maybe? She was a judge on the episode of *Ultimate Food Fighter* that you were on."

That caught Philippe's attention, and he stopped grating the cheese block. "Wait, Gianna Delano? She was here? In Paris? In Maison de Beauchene? Looking for me?"

"That was her name—Gianna Delano. Yep, she wanted to know if you were here." Penelope sounded so nonchalant.

Philippe asked, "Well, what did she want?"

His attention was a hundred percent focused on Penelope. She would've savored this, except it was for the wrong reason: that American woman.

At the same time, Arnauld happened to walk by and notice Philippe's paused position.

"Get to work, Deneuve!" Arnauld's voice boomed as he walked past, carrying a hot roasting pan full of a freshly cooked pork shoulder.

Penelope flashed Philippe a conniving smile and playfully hit his shoulder. "Yeah, get to work, Deneuve!"

Philippe got back to grating cheese but was dying to know more about their mysterious conversation. Why had Gianna been looking for him? "All right, Penelope, don't make me pry this out of you. Start talking!"

"Okay, okay. She said she thought your cooking was good and that she wanted you to be her new chef at some restaurant in Los Angeles. I think she's crazy. Who flies to a different country to proposition someone about a job? Hello? Hasn't the girl heard of e-mail?"

Philippe's heart stopped beating for a minute. He feared that Penelope had showed Gianna her devil side. "Please tell me that you were nice to her. She's a big deal."

He saw from the look on Penelope's face that his fear was true: she had been a jerk. Penelope wasn't a force that anyone wanted to reckon with.

"I mean, I probably could have been a little bit nicer. I told her that you weren't interested."

"*Penelope!*" Philippe shouted.

"Relax. She gave me her card and told me to pass it along." She fished it out of the back pocket of her black pants and handed it to him. "Here you go. Calm down now."

He took it and looked at the script of her name, Gianna Delano. He remembered how beautiful she'd looked the day he met her. If he had a Magic 8 Ball and asked it if he should call her, the silly toy would give him a response like, "Without a doubt" or "As I see it, yes" or even "Signs point to yes."

If nothing else came of it, Gianna was a networking contact.

"Are you going to call her?" Penelope asked.

"Probably. It's the polite thing to do." But Philippe was afraid that he had missed a golden opportunity.

She looked at him curiously. "You wouldn't actually move to America, would you?"

"I've never thought of it, that's for sure." But his dream was to run his own kitchen. He wanted to be the head chef, the guy calling the final shots on the menu details. The idea of relocating was—dare he say it?—exciting.

"She's staying at the Four Seasons. She said she would be here for a few days. Don't be mad, please?"

Philippe sighed. He didn't even want to know what Penelope had said to Gianna. A comfortable silence returned between her and co-worker. Philippe was furious at her, but she was like a naughty sibling; it was useless to scold her. Penelope would be Penelope. Yet accepting her for who she was didn't mean he wanted to talk to her all the time.

Arnauld came into the kitchen with news of an angry customer in the dining room. "At Table 12, there's a couple complaining that the fish was undercooked and the pasta was too crunchy. Go appease them, please, Philippe. It's a young couple. They'll respond better to you than to me."

"I'm on it!" Philippe put down his spatula.

"Oh, and they already ate their meals. Do not comp their food. We could have fixed it had they said they didn't like it after a bite or two, but they may as well have licked their plates clean!" Arnauld said with great displeasure and frustration.

Philippe could tell that the customers were annoyed before he even got to their table. They both had sour expressions, but Philippe knew exactly how to fix this situation. "Good evening, *monsieur et mademoiselle.* My name is Philippe Deneuve, and I am one of the chefs here. How was everything this evening?"

The man replied, "We're disappointed. We are here for our five-year wedding anniversary, and we heard this was the best place in Paris."

"Happy anniversary!" Philippe interjected.

"Thanks," he replied.

"I heard you were not quite pleased with the food, so here is what I am going to do. I'm going to bring you each one of our famous crème brules a celebratory dessert. It's our way of saying thanks for choosing Maison de Beauchene for your special dinner."

The young woman looked interested. "That sounds great. We'd love that!"

Philippe flashed his charming smile to seal the deal. "I'll bring it right out to you."

He went back to the kitchen and personally prepared the crème brulée. The dessert had been made earlier, so it just needed the final touches. He grabbed the kitchen torch, threw on a thick layer of white granulated sugar, and used the torch to crisp the top. He added a layer of powdered sugar, opened a container of raspberries, and carefully placed three berries on the dish. For the final touch, he garnished it with a sprig of mint leaf. Perfect!

He took it back out to the couple and presented it to them. "Here you are."

"Wow! This looks incredible," they both exclaimed.

Philippe knew that their Maison de Beauchene experience had just improved, but to make sure, he said, "Oh, and one more thing." He poured them two glasses of champagne. "Happy anniversary to a wonderful couple. If you need anything else, please ask for me by name: Philippe Deneuve."

"Thanks, Philippe!" The woman picked up a spoon, ready to dive face first into the mouth-watering dessert.

He left them to enjoy their fresh crème brulées, but he cast one final glance their way before heading into the kitchen. They were toasting and happy, which was exactly how every guest should leave their restaurant.

Philippe went back to working beside Penelope for the rest of the evening. He didn't utter a word to her.

While the guests might leave happy, he was one chef who would leave Maison de Beauchene with an attitude. All he wanted was to go home and drink a beer. He'd had a rough night and realized that he needed to make some serious changes in his life, stat.

CHAPTER FOUR

One of the perks of working in the restaurant business was being able to sleep through the mornings. One of the major cons was working nights and weekends.

This particular morning, Philippe had no complaints about a few extra Z's, especially because he had a case of the nerves. He planned to call Gianna, and the mere thought of explaining what he was sure was Penelope's horrifyingly wicked behavior made him want to put the pillow right over his face. His biggest trepidation was that she had blown his chance with Gianna before he even had a chance.

What do I have to lose? He pulled the card out of the pants he'd worn last night, which were lying on a chair. Gianna's email and phone number were listed on the card, and he would've loved to send her an email instead—the Internet was a wonderful place for cowardly behavior. But Philippe manned up and grabbed his cell phone. He punched the number into the phone.

After a three rings, someone picked up. "Gianna Delano speaking."

"Gianna? Hi." He spoke in English, which was a little rusty. "This is Philippe Deneuve. My co-worker told me you stopped by and gave me your card."

"Hi, Philippe." Her voice sounded cool.

"I think Penelope may have indicated that I wasn't interested in the position at your restaurant, but I would like a little more information."

"Thanks for getting back in touch, but I'm not sure the position is still available."

"Oh. That's too bad." Philippe was admittedly disappointed. He had been under the impression that Gianna had flown there just to talk to him. Clearly that wasn't the case.

"Do you want to meet for lunch, and maybe we can talk?" Gianna asked. "Even if this opportunity isn't an option?"

Unfortunately, Philippe didn't see it as a promising lead, and he didn't want to spend his day chasing unrequited dreams. "If the job's already filled, I don't want to waste your time. I'm thrilled to know you were interested in me as a potential candidate. Enjoy Paris!"

***

Stunned, Gianna said her good-byes and stared at her phone in disbelief after they hung up. What had just happened? She let out a roar of frustration, went to the closet to grab the fluffy white hotel robe, and put it on before crawling under the covers. Clearly playing hard to get hadn't been the right route to take. The whole point of coming to Paris was to convince Philippe to be her chef.

If only I hadn't made up the part about the job maybe being filled. Would he have been open to talking? I'll never know now.

Her phone beeped, and she hoped it was Philippe texting to say he'd changed his mind, but no, it was from her parents.

Hi sweetpea! Hope you're having fun in Paris! Love, Mom and Dad.

She exhaled a dramatic sigh of exasperation and sat up in bed. Not one to wallow and sit around, Gianna decided that she may as well have some fun. Hanging out in a hotel room wasn't exactly what someone should do when in Paris, or in any other beautiful city for that matter. She was away from home and adventures awaited.

Gianna thought of the Shakespeare quote, "The world is my oyster." Well, today, tomorrow, and the next day, Paris would be Gianna's oyster. When in Paris, right?

She couldn't let her parents down. They were so sweet, although she'd learned at an early age that her parents were different from her friends' parents. The best words to describe them were quirky and independent. Her dad, an inventor, created all kinds of projects. Many of them failed, yet he never got discouraged. He said every failed attempt put him one try closer to figuring out the right way to do it. He was a problem solver and a true optimist, qualities he's passed right along to Gianna.

Her first visit to Paris came right after he received a major patent for a robotic device that allowed doctors to do hands-free hip replacements. He'd asked Gianna where she wanted to go, and when she said Paris, he booked the trips for them and her mom, of course. They were the ultimate tourists with camera straps around their necks, maps, and many, many failed attempts at speaking French. Once, her mother accidentally asked for a dead fish instead of a soda. It was so funny. The memory made Gianna both laugh and cringe. After that trip, Gianna had started learning French, and it came in handy during her modeling career, which took her to megacities all over the world.

Gianna's mom was a knitter who loved being at home and sharing her creations and patterns on her very successful craft blog. She was an old soul, who preferred handwritten letters as a way of communication, so she didn't understand Gianna's desire to walk down runways dressed in haute couture or her ramblings about designers and their dramas. But she always supported Gianna.

If her parents knew that she was moping around in a hotel, they would be so disappointed. Besides, a little retail therapy always made her feel better, so her first stop was Avenue Montaigne. The street was covered with tourists and locals alike, and Gianna enjoyed blending in with the crowd, being an observer. She noticed that half of the street-strollers were simply window shopping for Prada, Dior, Jean Paul Gaultier, Givenchy, Chanel, Louis Vuitton, Gucci. Her closet was full of sample-sized dresses and makeup and perfume by all of those brands. She walked in and perused the stores, one by one. In each store, she was greeted warmly, probably because she looked like someone on a mission to spend all of her money.

After making it down a block's worth of shops, she stopped at cafe for tea. The cute tables were small and close together, and she grabbed a spot by the window. She ordered a green tea.

The cute guy at the table beside her had an espresso with a croissant, and he offered to buy her drink. "Excuse me, may I treat you to this?"

She turned to him. He was cute. Not as cute as Philippe, of course, but cute nonetheless.

"Sure, why not?"

Mystery Guy said, "I'm Thierry."

"Gianna." She smiled at him and took a sip of her tea.

"Are you here on vacation?"

"Just a little work travel," she said, which wasn't entirely untrue. Small talk had become a third language to her, but she had enough common sense to avoid telling a stranger that she was a tourist. You never knew who you could be talking to, although a little afternoon company in a quaint cafe seemed harmless enough. "What about you? You seem like a native Parisian."

"Good guess. You're right. I'm a design assistant, and I actually should be getting back. But when a women is as beautiful and poised as you, I had to say hello."

Gianna laughs. "Well, thanks."

"Do you think you'll have time for a longer coffee while you're here?" he asked.

"Maybe." She acted coy, but when he asked for her number, she gave it to him.

"While you're in town, you have to try Maison de Beauchene. It's the best in town," he said. "Maybe I'll take you there one day."

Oh, the irony. "I've heard of it."

They parted ways. Getting hit on wasn't unusual for her, but love was still a mystery. She couldn't say she had ever been properly in love. Men found her attractive, and sometimes she found them attractive, but love was more than physical attraction. She'd had a couple of long-term boyfriends, but she never saw any long-term potential with them and wasn't terribly heartbroken when each relationship ended. The kind of love she was after was the kind her parents had. A few of her friends had it too

She knew in her gut that this Thierry guy wasn't her guy. Maybe for a coffee or a dinner but not for the long haul. That kind of love only came around a few times in a person's lifetime. At this point, Gianna would be lucky to experience it once.

Maybe she was too busy, or simply not ready, but would she ever be in a position in her life when she wasn't busy? She would always be short on free time, especially with her restaurant opening up. Perhaps it was simply a matter of finding the right guy that she would actually want to make time for. She sighed and got up.

Gianna continued to peruse the designer shops, many of which resembled those on Rodeo Drive. She didn't buy anything, but she did try on a few things, including a deep purple dress that would be perfect for the soft opening of Chic, Mais Oui! She made a mental note to come back and get it if she still loved it before she left.

But no matter how many stores or how many people Gianna weaved among, she couldn't get Philippe Deneuve out of her mind. She had a feeling, a women's intuition kind of feeling, that he would be the perfect addition to her restaurant. He would be fun, the patrons would adore him, and she wondered what it would be like to work alongside him. She imagined that he would be goofy and flirty and fun. Was that how he was with Penelope? Did Gianna dare admit that she felt a hint of jealousy at that thought?

She tried to banish and squelch the emotion as she walked back to the Four Seasons. She took the slightly longer route so that she could stroll past Maison de Beauchene. She told herself that it wasn't stalking—she was just walking past a business to see what the dinner rush hour looked like. If she happened to catch a glimpse of Philippe, she wouldn't hate it, but Penelope, on the other hand? Gianna would be happy to never cross paths with that girl ever again.

The warm glow from the restaurant was inviting, and the place was jam-packed, as she could see from the windows. Right as she walked by the door, it opened, and she breathed in a whiff of heavenly food smells: fresh rolls, sweet desserts, perfectly grilled meat. She'd developed a nose for fine food, and that was it. No wonder Philippe had a hard time making the leap from this place to another.

Besides, how much fun was it to work with his significant other? Based on Penelope's reaction to her unexpected visit, Gianna was willing to bet all the euros in her wallet that she and Philippe were dating. Perhaps they were even married or engaged. Gianna had forgotten to check for any specific jewelry on Penelope's hand. Although she had no idea what Philippe saw in her. Sure, Penelope was pretty, but her personality? Yikes!

What you doing here? Gianna asked herself as she walked the final block to her hotel. While she was trying hard to enjoy her mini-vacation, she couldn't help but feel as though the entire trip was a complete and total waste of time.

The following day, Gianna tried to cheer herself up. After all, she was in Paris. She couldn't just sit around and mope.

She hit Musée de l'Orangerie, which she hadn't been to before. She finally saw Monet's *Water Lilies*. There were eight of them, huge canvases displayed in two oval white rooms. She felt as though she could sit and look at them all day, and she planned to, until her stomach growled.

She took the cue from her body and went to a local supermarket to buy typical French picnic food: a baguette, some cheese, and some wine. She took the Metro to the Eiffel Tower and sat on a bench in Champs de Mars. There, she people-watched and enjoyed a beautiful afternoon. Of course, she was also under the presence of the beautiful and iconic tower.

The solid, massive steel structure inspired strength in her; she decided that she might as well try to talk to Philippe one last time. She'd come there on a mission, and she should see it through. She'd rather go back home knowing that she had exhausted every possible outlet. It was what her dad would do.

She dialed Philippe's number and was surprised when he answered right away.

"Hello?"

"Philippe, it's Gianna Delano. Again."

"Hi! What can I do for you?"

"I'm still here in Paris, and I wanted to see if you would be willing to meet with me. The position at Chic, Mai Oui is available now, and I would love for you to be my new head chef. Are you interested?" Gianna squeezed her eyes shut and crossed her fingers, afraid and desperate to hear his answer.

"I'm interested."

"Wait, what?" Gianna wasn't sure she'd heard him correctly.

"Let's meet up and talk."

"Perfect."

They made arrangements for a meeting on Monday at his place.

I love this city. Gianna hung up and finished her picnic. Maybe her intuition was guiding her on the right path after all.

CHAPTER FIVE

The next day at Maison de Beauchene, as soon as Penelope walked in the door, Philippe ran over to her. "Penelope! Penelope!"

"Let me guess, you talked to Legs?" She rolled her eyes.

"Huh?"

Penelope rolled her eyes. "Legs! My nickname for Gianna."

"As a matter of fact, I did talk to *Gianna*. I have a good feeling about this, and I need your help, but only if you promise to actually help me."

"Oh, fine. What do you need?"

"On Monday, I'm having a few friends over," he said. "I'm going to make some of my best dishes and wow Gianna. It'll be a nice evening.

I want to show that I'm capable of cooking for a group of people and impressing them all. Can you help me by being my catering partner in crime? We make a good team, you and I."

"What's in it for me?"

"Hmm, let's see. My job? If I leave Maison de Beauchene, Arnauld would absolutely give you a promotion. You could be me," he teased, thumping his hands on his chest.

"Right, because everyone wants to be a Deneuve." Penelope rolled her eyes again.

Philippe shook his head. "Funny, funny."

"You're really tired of Maison de Beauchene, aren't you?"

"Arnauld is incredible. He's one of the best in the business. I can't deny it, you can't deny it, and if you ask him, he'll tell you that he's the best in the industry. He's more than a mentor. He's a friend. But you know me, I've been wanting to expand my creativity for a while now. Maison de Beauchene isn't the place to do it."

Penelope nodded. "I'll help you. Just remember that I really am a nice person."

"Thank you, Penelope. Really, I mean it. Thanks. And one more thing?"

She stopped folding napkins. "What's that?"

"For the love of all things good, could you please be on your best behavior? Not everyone gets your humor." He was treading carefully, trying not to hurt Penelope's feelings. Under her tough girl façade and never-ending sarcasm, he knew she was more sensitive than she would ever admit.

"Yeah, yeah, I get what you're saying. Be nice and don't scare your guests away. You're just using me for my cooking skills because you know I'm better at this gig than you."

Their witty banter wasn't really flirtatious. It was more like siblings' teasing.

"I knew this day would come."

Philippe and Penelope jumped when they heard the person behind them. Philippe wanted to bury his face in his hands. He hoped Arnauld hadn't heard all that.

"Give us a minute, will you, Penelope dear?" Arnauld waved her back to the kitchen.

"Sure." She headed toward the back of the restaurant.

"How much did you hear?" Philippe asked, nervous that his boss had heard any or all of it.

"Enough to know that you're ready."

"Ready for what?" Philippe cocked his head toward Arnauld.

"To be on your own."

Philippe noticed how old Arnauld seemed all of the sudden. Were those creases in his forehead new? What about the thinning hair?

"So you heard all of it," Philippe said.

"Enough." Arnauld smiled and smacked Philippe's back. "When I took you in, I knew you had something special. You reminded me of, well, me."

"Yeah?" Philippe smiled. That was a high compliment.

"I knew you wouldn't be here forever. I thought maybe one day you would take over Maison de Beauchene, but you have to grow and be your own chef. If you don't love it, the dishes you create are no longer art. Cooking is art; food is art. I'll always be here, and I'll always support you."

"So you aren't mad?"

"Not at all, dear boy. Just be sure to remember me when you have your own famous restaurant."

"I will."

"For now, you're not the top man yet. So into my kitchen you go," Arnauld teased, gave Philippe a wink, and ushered him into the kitchen to prep for tonight's crowd. "Oh, and Philippe?"

Philippe turned to look back at Arnauld. "Yes, sir?"

"No matter what happens or where you go or how far you go, I'll always be your friend. I'll always be your mentor. You're like a son to me, you know that?"

Philippe was touched by the old man's words. He smiled and nodded. Sometimes, words didn't have a place in the conversation.

Philippe felt a wave of relief, and all of the sudden, his work there seemed better than it had in weeks. Maybe things weren't as bad as he had thought. No matter how much someone liked their job, there were always rough patches. Maybe this was just a rough patch for Philippe. In order to appreciate the good, you had to endure the not-so-good, right?

As Philippe got back to work, he couldn't stop thinking about what his boss had said. Did Arnauld really think Philippe could take over Maison de Beauchene one day? Was that better than Gianna's offer? The question lingered in his mind and made him even more anxious for Monday's dinner meeting.

***

Early Monday morning, Penelope met Philippe at his house to go over the menu. They were splitting up the grocery shopping, then they would get started cooking right away.

"Why didn't you do the shopping yesterday?" Penelope whined, searching his kitchen for coffee beans.

"I wanted to get the freshest ingredients possible."

"Well, I won't leave until I've had my caffeine," Penelope demanded.

Philippe sighed. "Fine." He made a shot of espresso from his machine.

"Mmm." Penelope was clearly not a morning person, especially not on her day off.

Philippe shook his head. "You don't need coffee, Penny. You're high-strung enough without caffeine flowing through your veins. I gave you decaf."

A look of pure horror overcame Penelope's face. "You didn't!"

Philippe flashed her one of his mischievous grins. "I did."

"A decaf espresso? I didn't even know that existed!"

Chloe Emile

He gave Penelope her half of the list and a small wad of euros. "Meet back here in an hour?"

Philippe was in charge of getting the bulk of food ingredients, and he was trusting Penelope to get fresh flowers, wine, and cheese.

"I'm keeping the change so I can buy real coffee," Penelope said before leaving.

***

"The place looks great." Penelope walked around the dining room and finished setting the table, even though the dinner was still a few hours away.

Just like at the restaurant, they worked seamlessly together. They didn't even need to talk; they could intuitively tell what the other needed. So instead of conversing, Philippe turned up the music and hummed along to the tune.

About half an hour before his few friends and the guest of honor, Gianna, were supposed to show up, Philippe dressed up for the occasion, and put the final touches on the party details. He lit some candles then put on upbeat music for ambiance. While it may be a fun get-together for his friends, it was an audition for him.

His brother Mathieu and his wife, Violette, were the first guests to arrive, followed by four other good friends, an even mixture of women and men. Philippe charmed them with his perfect hospitality, taking jackets and pouring drinks.

"So did you win?" Mathieu asked him.

"Ultimate Food Fighter? You know I can't tell you that. I'm under contract not to say anything until the episode airs."

"Come on, it won't even air here in France. Who are we going to tell?"

Philippe shrugged and mimed zipping his lips.

"So tell us a little bit more about the girl then," Violette said, smiling.

Everyone leaned in a little closer, eager to hear that story. They were all vaguely aware that Gianna was a restaurateur who was interested in hiring Philippe. Penelope perked up as Philippe told them about her judging the television show in Los Angeles and that she was a model.

"I think he has a little thing for her," Penelope added.

"Is she hot?" Clement, one of his buddies, asked.

"Of course she is," Simon said. "She's a model."

"So what's she like?"

He was just about to answer when... saved by the bell! The doorbell rang, and there was a faint, dainty knock on his door.

There she was, the last to show up. Philippe's jaw dropped when he opened the door and saw Gianna. She was stunning. There was no other word for it. She wore a lovely black dress, and her hair and makeup were flawless. Her long honey-colored hair went down to her waist in gentle curls. She stepped inside and waved hello to the other guests. Everyone stopped and stared, even Penelope.

"Hey! Hi, come on in." Philippe kissed Gianna swiftly on both cheeks, and a little jolt of electricity ran through him when his lips touched her soft, impeccably made-up cheeks. "What can I get you to drink?"

"Red wine? Any will work." She flashed him a smile, and he knew he was in trouble. Big, big trouble.

He poured a glass and handed it to her.

"Hi, everyone, I'm Gianna," she said in French.

There was a murmur of hellos, and Philippe made introductions all around. Penelope hung out in the background, the wallflower, and watched as the guys gaped at Gianna and the girls doted on her.

"Thanks. Gosh, everything looks so nice." Gianna looked around the living room and smiled at Philippe's friends.

"Penelope helped," Philippe said. "I'm going to check on something in the kitchen. I'll be back out in a second."

Philippe went back to check on his food, leaving Gianna to mingle with his friends. It might've been a small crowd, but Gianna seemed to have already bewitched every single person in the room. Any hot-blooded male would think that she was beyond gorgeous. As for the women, they asked her all sorts of questions about her clothes and makeup, so they must've liked her sense of style. He was relieved that things were going smoothly right off the bat.

Penelope and Philippe brought out some appetizers, including *pissaladiere, vorschmack*, a vegetable *pyttipannu*, and fresh baguette slices with a myriad of dips and spreads, including an asparagus-walnut pesto. Gianna made an effort to try a taste of each item, and each sample reminded her of why she'd flown out there. Everything Philippe made was spectacular. She saw fireworks with every bite, and she told him so.

"Don't give me all the credit. Penelope worked on these as well." Penelope beamed at him, but her smile quickly turned to scorn when Philippe spoke again. "Tonight, I want to make a special toast to the beautiful and unbelievably sweet Gianna Delano. Our shindig tonight is in your honor, and we are happy you are here to share a meal with all of us."

Gianna blushed, and everyone raised their glasses to clink with one another. As the wine flowed and the appetizers were devoured, Philippe announced that it was almost time for the main event: dinner. The company was fun, even despite Penelope. She couldn't remember the last time she'd gone to a dinner party and felt immediately comfortable. A lot of her close friends were in the fashion industry, and dinner parties usually required her to be on and to schmooze.

But tonight was perfect. She was chatting with Violette and the other girls like old friends. And the food! Gianna wanted the night to go on forever. The party alone was worth the plane ticket.

CHAPTER SIX

$\mathcal{E}$veryone stood and started making their way to the dining room. Well, almost everyone. One person was trying to stand but was failing. Just when she looked as though she was upright, she plopped back onto the couch, hiccupping.

"Oh no," Aria said. "It looks like Penelope has gone from tipsy to flat-out drunk."

"Nah-uh. I'm just having fun. This is a party after all." Penelope sounded defensive as she slurred her words. Once she managed to make her way to the dining room, she loudly declared, "This party would be so much better without the funny-looking American. We should take her to the airport right now and shred her passport so she can't ever come back." She laughed, apparently finding herself quite hilarious.

Silence settled over the room, and everyone turned to stare at the laughing hyena that was Penelope. Color filled Gianna's cheeks, and she looked down.

"I'm so sorry for Penelope's behavior," Philippe said. "This is inexcusable. Truly."

Gianna gracefully said everything was fine.

"Penelope. Living room. Now," Philippe ordered. When she didn't fall in line, he grabbed her wrist and pulled her into the other room. Once in the other room, Philippe yelled in a whisper, "What are you doing? Have you lost your mind? You are being completely unprofessional and just a mean, rude human being." He could tell Penelope was too drunk to care, however.

He was right. She laughed.

"You will go in there and apologize to Gianna at once."

Penelope laughed again. "I won't do it."

"Yes. Yes, you will."

The fierce look in Philippe's eyes must've conveyed how serious and angry he was because she meekly agreed. They walked back into the dining room, where everyone was already seated.

"Sorry," Penelope spat at Gianna.

"We've all had our moments." She smiled mercifully at the woman.

Penelope slinked into a chair and sat silently, sipping water. There was no chance her water would turn into wine.

"You have outdone yourself, Philippe," Violette said. "We haven't even gotten to the main course yet, but Gianna would be a lucky, lucky girl if she could get her hands on you–er, I mean your cooking."

Everyone laughed.

"Yes, Philippe," Gianna said. "You didn't have to go to this much trouble."

"It's my pleasure," Philippe said.

"I helped too. This isn't just his work, you know," Penelope said quietly.

Violette said, "You're right, Penelope. We haven't given you enough credit. You two threw together a wonderful party. We're happy to be here."

Penelope responded with a satisfied nod. It was so obvious that she was envious of all of the attention being lavished upon the exquisite model. But what should she expect? The party was in Gianna's honor, after all.

Philippe came out of the kitchen and said it would be just a few more minutes. He apologized for the wait. The fingerling potatoes weren't quite done, and Philippe was starting to feel as though the whole night was one giant failure. If he couldn't get food out for a group of eight, how could Gianna have confidence in him for a crowd at Chic, Mais Oui!?

Still, it was clear that Gianna was the group's darling. They asked her dozens of questions, but she didn't seem to mind one bit. She didn't just talk about herself but asked the questions right back. Philippe's friends were an interesting bunch, and they shared one hilarious story after another. He could see that Gianna was getting comfortable again. When the topic reverted back to Gianna's modeling career, she seemed more than happy to answer Aria's question.

"I got scouted when I was fifteen. It was something I did after school and on weekends. I guess I was a mid-tier model, you could say. Still am, really."

"You're being modest," Aria said. "I'm pretty sure I've seen you in magazines. You look very familiar. What kind of campaigns have you done recently?"

Gianna told them about the jewelry campaign she shot for an ethical diamond company. Later, she told stories about her life in the United States and about her parents. She told them about her dad's wacky inventions and how he'd made it big with his robot that performed surgery, although it was originally intended to walk the dog. They also found it amusing that her mother had a knitting blog.

"I've been thinking of taking up knitting," Simon joked. "Maybe I'll check it out."

Penelope threw a question at her out of nowhere. "So how do you go from model to restaurant-owner wannabe?"

As Gianna explained that she was basically a self-made woman looking to transition from the runway to Chic, Mais Oui!, Philippe eavesdropped from the kitchen. He lapped up every single last word of her adorably accented French. Maybe, just maybe, working for Gianna would be the best fit for him. He was almost ready to book his tickets. Then the timer beeped, and he got back to work.

"I hoped you don't mind me saying this," Violette said, "but your accent is so charming."

"French lessons might be helpful," Penelope said sharply. "I didn't catch all that."

Gianna blushed, but as usual, she ignored her new enemy's unnerving pokes.

Philippe called from the kitchen, "Be nice! You're doing great, Gianna. But I bet all Americans aren't nearly as alluring as you, right?" Philippe gave Penelope another warning look. He cursed Penelope in his mind and prayed that she would shut her mouth for the rest of the night.

"Geez, can't you take a joke? I'm just teasing her," Penelope claimed, though no one appeared to believe her. "You see, if I was going to be mean, I would tell Little Miss Princess Pants how stupid and awful her restaurant name is. Seriously, who puts an exclamation mark at the end of their restaurant name? It's like she's trying to be cute and French while sounding like a moron!"

Mouths opened, and everyone only stared at the train wreck that was Penelope.

"Chic, Mais Oui!" Penelope mocked with an exaggerated accent. "Or we can try it like this—Chic, Mais Oui! Chic, Mais Oui!" That time, she imitated Gianna's French accent. When she was done, she smirked at Gianna.

No one knew how to stop Penelope's madness. Gianna was growing more frustrated by the minute, yet she remained poised. She questioned Philippe's sanity and taste, though. If he wanted to be with someone like Penelope, then perhaps he wasn't a good fit for her. She swiftly changed her thoughts. Perhaps Philippe wasn't a good fit for her restaurant.

CHAPTER SEVEN

*I*t is before the lunchtime rush, so the quintessential French bistro isn't terribly crowded yet. Violette scans the place and sees two potential "Luc Deneuves" in the restaurant. The question is which one she should approach. She knows she needs to make a split-second decision.

"Gianna, oh my gosh, this is awful." Aria looked at Gianna with a bewildered expression.

"Yeah," the guy sitting beside her said. "Listen, this is just Penelope. All of us are used to her dramatics."

Penelope angrily took a sip of water before crossing her arms and fuming.

Mathieu, Philippe's brother, added, "Penelope is an incredible chef, she really is. However, all of her histrionics is the very reason why she'll never be as successful as Philippe."

"Wait a minute!" Penelope interjected. His comment seemed to sober her up rather quickly.

"No, you've said enough," Simon told her.

When Penelope tried to get another word in, she was cut off once again.

Philippe walked in with a couple of plates. On each plate sat an entrée trio platter with grilled whole branzino, butternut squash and pumpkin ravioli, and roasted chicken with fingerling potatoes. "What did I miss? The kitchen vent was on so I didn't hear everything."

Nervous glances were exchanged.

"Seriously, what did I miss?" He looked right at Penelope.

Mathieu was the bearer of bad news. "Penny here was just being Penny."

"Thanks a lot," she retorted. "You're my least favorite Deneuve."

"Just stop already," Philippe said. "Please, Penelope? This is getting out of hand."

Penelope nodded as if she were an obedient child.

Gianna wanted to draw the crowd's attention away from Penelope's comments and herself. She was there for the food and the food only. "Philippe, tell us what's on the menu."

"Happily."

Everyone oohed and ahhed with happy tummies as they talked about the wine pairings and raved over Philippe's mastermind. Unfortunately, the comfortable vibe from appetizers had suffered a slight shift.

"Okay, I need to grab one more thing." Philippe returned to the kitchen

In the dining room, Gianna said, "This looks so good. I can't wait to try all of it."

Murmurs and echoes of agreement came from all corners of the table, even from Penelope. Gianna let out a sigh she hadn't realized she was holding in. The evening could only go up from here. Right?

Wrong.

"There's no way that your American palate can be sophisticated enough to enjoy this. Don't we need to pick you up some French fries?" Penelope laughed at her joke.

Several of the guys groaned.

"Here we go again," Mathieu muttered.

"Seriously, I'm not being mean. I'm genuinely asking. How do you plan on being a restaurateur of a French restaurant?" Penelope asked.

The guests held their breaths. As if on cue, Philippe walked back into the dining room with the final platter.

"No, I'm being *nice*," Penelope said to Gianna. "I'm just saying that you will clearly need help. You should hire Philippe immediately. His cooking is mediocre but should be more than sufficient for a has-been model." Penelope looked pleased with herself. When Philippe gave her yet another warning look, she told him, "I was just trying to help you, get you hired."

"I think you all will need to excuse me. I'm actually going to be on my way." Gianna took the napkin off her lap and placed it gingerly on the table. "It was nice meeting all of you. Good night."

Philippe put down the plate and rushed after her. "Gianna, wait!"

"I'm sorry, Philippe, but I have enough self-respect to not let another person berate me and tear me down like that."

"Please don't go. Please. Penelope's behavior..." He grabbed Gianna's wrist, but she pulled it away. "Penelope has a weird sense of humor."

Why is he defending her? I guess love really does blind some people. With that thought, she willed herself to keep her focus on the door.

"So what's next?" Philippe asked hopelessly.

"What's next is I'm leaving."

She turned toward the door. After grabbing her jacket and her clutch, she reached for the doorknob. Just one twist of the knob would set her free. She had been served a hefty dose of ridicule and humiliation, and she was simply unable to suffer anymore. All of this had been a giant mistake. Paris was a stupid idea, and all she wanted to do was go home.

Home for now would be her hotel room. To her luck, she was able to snag a taxicab. After she gave the driver the address for the Four Seasons, she sighed. A teardrop, followed by another, fell down her cheek. Never in her life had she been treated so awfully, and she worked in the modelling industry!

The driver glanced in the rearview mirror. "Are you okay, *mademoiselle*?"

"I just had a bad night." She didn't want to talk about it. She pulled out her phone and played with it, hoping the cabbie would get the message and let her ride in silence.

Fortunately, it was a short drive. She could have walked, but she didn't want to walk even half a mile in Manolo Blahnik heels. The highlight of Gianna's night was when the driver pulled up to the hotel door. She paid him, tipping him well, and thanked him.

As he drove away, she walked into her temporary home. She was so upset that she didn't even pay attention to her hungry, rumbling stomach. But when the doorman opened the door for her, her stomach growled so loudly that she was positive he could hear it. *How embarrassing!*

She didn't even want to think about food. Instead, she took her bad attitude straight to bed. She crawled under the covers and pulled the blankets tightly around her, curling up in a little ball. Gianna felt like a complete and total fool. As she lay there, she replayed the events of the evening in her mind. Philippe's friends had been awesome, but she couldn't believe Philippe was dating Penelope. She was awful! But Philippe was an excellent cook, and she would still love to have him on board at her restaurant.

With that conclusion, she resolved to hurry to get a concrete yes or no from Philippe Deneuve. If it was a no, she could stop wasting her time.

Rumble. There went her stomach again. All Gianna wanted to do was sleep for a little bit. It wasn't that late, so maybe she'd wander out later. Room service got old after a while. For now, she sulked and had a pity party for one.

CHAPTER EIGHT

*T*he fiasco of a dinner party ended prematurely. After Gianna left, Philippe could have killed Penelope. He walked back into the dining room, and it was clear that the good mood had officially been murdered. Penelope stared at her plate. After quickly finishing his meal, Mathieu stood and announced that he and Violette should probably be heading out.

"Don't you want to stay and eat?" Philippe said. "Seriously, I have a ton of food."

Penelope picked up her fork and took a bite of the pumpkin and butternut squash ravioli. "The ravioli is amazing." She looked at Philippe with an expression that conveyed *I know I messed up big time.*

"I'll deal with you in a little while," he curtly replied.

She took another bite of ravioli.

Simon gestured all the dishes on the table then at Penelope. "It sounds like you have a mess to take care of, no pun intended."

"At least take some dessert to go." Philippe didn't give them the chance to say no before he went into the kitchen and cut slabs of tiramisu. He placed the slices in containers and carried them back to his friends. "Here you go." He handed the dessert to each of them, except for Penelope.

"Was Gianna okay?" Aria asked, taking the tiramisu.

"Eh, of course she was upset. I hope she's okay, but I have a feeling that I really blew it." He didn't bother to hide his anger, throwing a sharp look Penelope's way.

"I'll be honest, Philippe. Gianna seemed fantastic. Give her a chance to give you a chance." Violette put on her coat.

He let her comment soak in. *Give her a chance to give you a chance.* "I hope you're right."

Once the crew had left, Philippe closed the door. He was left alone with Penelope. She sat at the dining room table in the exact same spot she'd been in since she moved from the couch. She hadn't stopped staring at her empty plate for the past fifteen minutes.

In a low, growling voice, Philippe broke the silence. "Why did you do that?"

Penelope got sarcastic again. "I'm sorry, but seriously? That stupid American just didn't understand French humor."

Philippe put his hands on his hips and watched her with utter disbelief. He honestly had no idea what to make of her.

"Come on, I'm sorry," Penelope said. "I took the teasing too far. But look at all of this food we have. It would be a shame to let it all go to waste, don't you think?" She walked over to Philippe.

"What are you doing?" he asked.

"I was going to rub your back. You're tense and need to relax. It was one night."

While Philippe couldn't deny he was indeed stressed and in need of a good back rub, there was no way he'd accept anything from Penelope. Oh no, not tonight. He may find women irresistible, but he had no qualms about ignoring her coquettishness.

"You don't get it, do you?" He raised his voice, something he rarely did. He usually tried to blow off his anger and keep smiling, but tonight, Penelope had unleashed a rare anger in him.

Penelope jumped back, startled. "Stop already."

Philippe threw his hands in the air. He took a plate with the entrée trios and warmed it in the microwave. He sat at the table, choosing a seat as far away from Penelope as possible, and took a bite of chicken. God, it was good. *If only Gianna had tried this, I could have woken up tomorrow to a brand new life.*

"Do you remember the day we met?" Penelope asked.

He couldn't answer because his mouth was full of food, but he nodded, still refusing to look at her.

"I was so nervous starting at Maison de Beauchene. I couldn't believe Arnauld took a chance on me. It was a dream job for someone fresh out of culinary school. That first night, you were so charming."

"I know the story, Penelope. I was there. What is your point?"

"Just wait. We've had so many good times. You can't throw it all away over one... episode."

When Philippe didn't say anything, she continued her walk down memory lane. "You told me you liked my hat, which was crazy because we were wearing the exact same white coat and white hat, our uniform." She laughs. "Then you told me that we should have a rhubarb chopping competition. I beat you."

Philippe finally let his gaze meet hers. "That is because I let you win."

"I thought it was the start of something new, something good."

Philippe had thought so too. In fact, the two of them had dated for a very brief period. They had the same wonky schedule, and their dates often involved breakfast or lunch and a matinee instead of the traditional dinner and a movie. Neither of them could deny that they had chemistry, but Philippe thought they had the chemistry of siblings. Penelope had even met the Deneuve clan and visited his parents' home in Montmartre for one of his birthday parties. Shortly after that, Penelope and Philippe had had an argument over something stupid at work. Philippe couldn't even remember what it was about now.

However, Penelope had gotten scared of how potentially serious their relationship could get, which she admitted to him later. She was afraid he would lose interest in her one day, as other men had, so that night after work, she told him she wanted a break. Philippe had been relieved, because he didn't think they had a chance as a couple. However, because he knew her past, he remained more sensitive to her than others.

Penelope had a rough start in life. Her mother was addicted to cocaine and meth, and she would do anything for a fix, including making meth while Penelope tried to study in the next room. While her mother inhaled and injected herself with poison, her father drank his. Penelope was shocked his liver still functioned. A fifth of liquor was all he consumed for the first half the day. She hated her mother, loathed her father, and promised herself that she would be better.

The hovel of a place that Penelope's family had called home in the gritty Parisian suburbs was crawling with rats and roaches and often lacking in food. What little food did exist in the Solomon household was a luxury. So she began experimenting, cooking meals for one and doing her best to stay out of her parents' way. If she caught them at the wrong moment, she might end up with a black eye or belt marks on her behind.

As soon as she was able, she fled, put herself through culinary school on an academic scholarship, and landed in Arnauld's palm. He had become a father figure to her. Philippe had become close enough to almost be family as well.

He could see that Penelope was fearful of change. If he left, she would have no one else in her life who cared about her as much as he did, even if it was in a brotherly way.

Philippe sat beside Penelope and took her hand. "I'm incredibly angry at you right now. I will always be here for you, but I need to make one thing very clear here. I don't want to hurt you, but I refuse to lead you on. Yes, once we had something, but we are just friends, now and forever. There will never be an us."

Plump tears fell from her eyes like a waterfall, which was how she normally got her way, at least with Philippe.

"*Chérie*, the tears won't work this time."

"What if we are meant to be?" She wiped a tear with her cloth napkin.

"Then what's meant to be will work out in time, but I don't want you to hold on to false hope. We make a good team in the kitchen, but could you really imagine us as husband and wife?"

Penelope laughed. "You're really mad right now, aren't you?" Penelope stated that as more of a fact than a question.

"You just tried to sabotage my career. Of course I'm mad. What else would you expect? You knew this was a major opportunity for me. Even if it didn't work out, Gianna would've been an amazing contact. All of that is gone. You blew it all for me."

"No. That is far, far from the truth. I was just teasing her. She's just too dumb to get French humor."

"She isn't even here, and you won't stop bashing her! It's not that she doesn't get French humor. It's that she doesn't get you. Nobody gets you," he said.

"Ouch. That was harsh."

"Be nice. Try it and see what happens. If I leave, Arnauld won't give you my job unless you shape up and start acting like a decent human being."

"I don't want your job," she argued, although that was a bold lie. Of course she wanted his job.

Arnaud was aging, and they both knew that he needed a replacement. If Philippe was out of the running, Penelope would be next in line to take over the entire restaurant.

She started to realize that, so she decided to play nice. Maybe Philippe had a point about the whole good girl act. *Meet the new and improved Penelope Solomon.* "Fine, I messed up. I just... Philippe, I'll miss you if you leave me."

"Friends don't just disappear, Penny."

"I promise you. I promise you that I'll make nice with the American—I mean Gianna."

"I have a feeling it's too late."

His sadness was so visible that Penelope felt her heart crack for both him and herself, for a brief second at least. "Well, I have a feeling she'll come around. Don't give up yet."

"I think that's the first nice thing you've said all night. If you keep up the less temperamental side, your career could reach a new high as well."

There was a teasing tone to Philippe's advice, but it royally annoyed Penelope. She hid her ire by feigning a yawn. "All right, it's getting late. I'm getting out of here. Have fun with the dishes."

CHAPTER NINE

Of course she would leave me with dishes.
Philippe carried the last of the plates
into the kitchen and looked around. He sighed
dramatically. So much for having a catering
partner.

He knew Penelope was hurt and having
a hard time with the thought of change. The
one thing he didn't know was why she'd tried
to sabotage his night when she knew how
important it was to him. He has always been
there for her, but she couldn't even give him
one night? He never asked for favors. He was
the agreeable one, the one who went with the
flow, middle-child style.

He felt he deserved this opportunity with Gianna. He had worked hard. He had passion and ambition. He showered the world around him with attention, but he wanted the spotlight once in a while. His brothers and sisters, both older and younger, always seemed to get the most attention. The older ones gained attention for being the first-born kids, the trailblazers. The younger kids needed homework help, and they were cuter. But the middle kids like Philippe? He was the observant one.

However, he had realized early on that girls loved him. They couldn't and still couldn't resist the dimple in his left cheek or his honey-brown eyes. His riotous curls were just the icing on the cake. Over the years, he had found his good looks to be both a blessing and a curse. Every chance he got to speak with a woman was a chance to flirt. He was too down-to-earth to be overbearing, but he had learned that women liked to feel beautiful, intelligent, and desired.

Sometimes that made him prone to extravagant displays of affection for the women he dated. He'd been known to lead girls on. His interest was piqued easily, but he lost that same interest just as quickly. A long-term relationship was elusive to him. As much as he adored women, he couldn't find a woman to truly fall in love with.

He wanted the love his parents had. His mother and father were so different, his father being a type A, practical businessman and his mother being a hippie artist. Yet somehow they just fit together. Philippe had dated many women, but he couldn't see himself marrying and loving any of them for the rest of his life. Maybe it was because he was young and just wanted to have fun, but deep down, he knew that wasn't true. All he needed was the right woman, and he would adore and cherish her for the rest of his days. Would that woman be Gianna?

As he opened the dishwasher, he wondered if Gianna had seen any charm in him. He didn't think so, but maybe that was just the American way. Was there a chance she was just playing hard to get? He wanted to do something to make up for tonight, but he wasn't sure what his next move should be with that particular woman. If she was going to be his potential business partner, he couldn't mess it up by flirting with her.

Sure, Gianna was beautiful, but he had met plenty of beautiful women in his lifetime. There were plenty of them in Paris. But the girl from Los Angeles had something special. Maybe it was her collected calm, her ambition, her passion for food. He could tell she was a hard worker. Maybe some people couldn't see it because she was a model, but he admired that she was practical enough to save money to go on to pursue her dream. Opening a restaurant was no small feat. Gianna was braver than he was to take the risk.

He also found it exciting that she wanted a French fusion restaurant. If only he could be a part of it. If only he could get to know her better.

He put the silver in the holder, then he put the leftovers in Tupperware so he could stick those plates in the dishwasher next. As he rinsed the plates before putting them in the dishwasher, his thoughts wandered back to Gianna.

What would it be like to kiss her? The thought sent a chill over his body. He thought of her long legs, sculpted body, and beautiful long hair. He was a lover of all things exquisite, and Gianna was definitely exquisite. The thought of being more than mere acquaintances with her was intoxicating, but he knew that scenario meant walking a very, very thin line.

He once saw a guy on TV walking across a tightrope over the mountains. If he were to fall, he would have died. That was what would happen if Philippe started working for Gianna and hooked up with her too. There would be nothing to catch him if he fell. But when he thought about her and her charming comments with her cute accent, taking the risk of falling sounded more enticing.

Then he realized it might not even be an option. Gianna had gone home feeling absolutely humiliated.

"Penelope!" He groaned to release his frustration as he wiped down the counters and blew out the candles. "Tomorrow. Tomorrow, I will call Gianna and win her over."

He swept the kitchen and imaged what it would be like to sweep while Gianna held the dustpan. They would have so much fun working alongside each other. With her witty jokes and his flirtations, it would never feel like a day of actual work. They would collaborate on the menu, and he would wow her with his creativity and divine cooking. They would look amazing in magazine articles and news clips. They would be the ultimate power couple.

His vision of a French modern fusion restaurant could come to life. No more Arnauld telling him to be more traditional, telling him to do it the Maison de Beauchene way. Philippe loved the idea of a red, black, and white theme for Chic, Mais Oui! He even liked the idea of having black-and-white French movies projected onto screens on the wall as part of the ambiance. He pictured the lines of people waiting. A bouncer would have to turn people away. Reservations would be impossible to get because the place would stay so booked.

The more he thought about it, the more he desperately wanted to know what Gianna's vision was. He knew it was a modern French cuisine with a classy vibe. Would they have the same tastes and ideas?

He wished she were there with him as he pulled out the last two pieces of tiramisu. One for him and one meant for Gianna. He didn't even bother to get a plate—he ate right out of the pan. The idea of cleaning one more dish seemed repulsive.

Oh, Gianna. He couldn't stop thinking about her. An image of sharing this dessert with her popped into his mind. That thought faded when he realized that he had never told Gianna how much he was actually interested in the job.

"Stupid," he cursed himself.

He was pretty sure her answer would be no anyway. She probably thought he was awful for being associated with Penelope. Of course she wouldn't be interested in hiring him.

But he would absolutely call her. If he had to, he would grovel. She had come all the way to Paris, partly to invite him to apply for the job. He should've made her feel more welcome, but he'd done the complete opposite of that.

"Why, Penelope, why?"

He turned out the lights. He had extra energy to burn, and all the caffeine he'd drunk was still running strong in him, so he pulled a gray sweater over his button-up shirt and went for a walk. Fresh air and exercise could make a man feel whole again.

The night air was crisp, as it could only feel in May. Warm and sunny days with chilly nights, or sweater weather as his mom would call it. His neighborhood wasn't the most exciting, so he hailed a cab and got off at Champs-Ely-sees. Even though there were always plenty of tourists there, he liked the street. It was beautiful at night, and it was a great place to people-watch. He usually saw interesting hustlers and street performers, especially during tourist season. Since none of his friends would go there, it was a great place for him to be alone without worrying about running into anyone he knew.

He wandered around to take his mind off things. The avenue wasn't as crowded as usual, which surprised him, but he didn't mind. He couldn't shake off the feeling that someone was watching him though. He looked behind him but didn't see anything out of the ordinary.

Maybe it was all those crime shows he had been watching.

One thing he had learned from growing up in Paris was that it was one of the most magical cities in the world. He loved it, and if by chance he did move to the United States, a piece of his heart would always be right here. He loved the history represented by the Arc de Triumph, the enormousness of the Louvre. He had gone to that museum dozens of times but still hadn't made a dent in the galleries. He'd come to locate some hidden nooks and crannies where his favorite paintings and artwork were usually located though. He wondered if Gianna would like to go with him.

He was starting at the southeast side of the street, walking away from the Arc. Living within walking distance of this beautiful tree-lined boulevard was a blessing. If he went to the end and back, he could get in a good eight kilometers. It would help him walk off some dessert calories at least. When he passed the intersection for Avenue George V, he turned down it instead of going straight. Gianna's hotel was down this street, and the idea of being close to her was vitalizing.

Wait, am I being creepy?

He saw the white exterior of the Four Seasons and walked by slowly, marveling at its beauty and architecture. He walked a few blocks past the hotel and turned around. When he got back to the door, low and behold, Gianna was walking through it. He saw the doorman checking her out and felt a jealous zing, which was crazy.

When she didn't see him, he almost walked past her. What kind of excuse could he give? *Oh, I was just walking by your hotel. Thought I'd catch you this fine evening!* They all sounded lame.

Maybe it was fate, maybe it was subconscious inclination, but even though he decided not to say anything, his mouth had a mind of its own. "Gianna?"

Startled, she looked confused for a second. "Philippe! Hi. What are you doing over here?"

"I was out for a walk, enjoying the night."

She clearly wasn't buying it. "By my hotel?"

"Champs-Elysees is one of my favorite streets in Paris. I was just extending the walk by coming down this street. I promise I'm not stalking you or anything." He laughed nervously, which only made him sound like even more of a weirdo creep. *Great, just great.*

"Oh, well..." Gianna certainly seemed to be more aloof than earlier.

"Look, this is awkward. Tonight was awkward. Penelope is really sorry for how she acted. Can you give me another chance?"

Gianna squinted and pursed her lips, seeming unsure of what to say. He braced himself for her reaction.

CHAPTER TEN

*I*t turned out, Philippe was right—he just didn't know it. Somebody was following him and watching his interaction with Gianna. Penelope sat on a nearby bench, pretending to read the newspaper. She rolled her eyes with disgust as she overheard what he told the American. *What is it about this girl that Philippe likes so much?*

"This is more than just awkward. Gianna, I want to make this right. Don't let Penelope give you the wrong idea about French people. I promise, she's a rare breed. Most people here are nothing like her. I'm not giving excuses for her, but she hasn't exactly had the easiest life."

Gianna crossed her arms.

Philippe could tell that his apology didn't resonate with her as much as he had hoped. "Do you mind if I ask where you are going?"

"I'm just getting some air." As she spoke, her stomach grumbled loudly. It sounded like an uneven dryer going *thump, thump, thump.* She hoped Philippe didn't notice.

"I was thinking about grabbing a bite of dinner. Care to join me?" *Please say yes, please say yes.* He saw her hesitation, but he refused to take no for an answer. He hooked his arm around hers. "Come on, I have a plan."

When he flashed his adorable, heart-melting, pulse-stopping smile, she gave in.

Philippe didn't actually have a plan, but he figured some café or bistro would speak to him when they passed it. They walked in silence, soaking in the moonlight, arms linked together. The city lights made the stars impossible to see, but he knew they were there. When they were about a block away from Maison de Beauchene, Philippe had a brilliant idea that was like a giant light bulb going off in his mind.

"Come on!" He unlinked his arm and grabbed her hand, pulling her down a little side street that would be considered a sketchy alley in America.

"Where are we going?" Gianna asked, sounding alarmed.

"We're going to Maison de Beauchene, just through the back entrance. I'm asking for a second chance for my audition."

Philippe knew he was breaking the rules. Arnauld didn't let anyone mess in his kitchen unless he was there. Having her in the restaurant after hours and without permission was definitely against the kitchen commandments. For all Philippe knew, he was breaking the law. *Arnauld would understand, right?*

They might be the famous last words, but what Arnauld didn't know wouldn't hurt him. All Philippe knew was he absolutely, positively must make tonight up to Gianna. She should never have had to deal with Penelope's terrible treatment of her.

He found the restaurant key on his key ring and jangled it into the lock. The restaurant was closed on Mondays, which was why he and Penelope had both had the night off and why the building was empty.

Having seen one too many Hollywood horror movies, Gianna shivered, a little nervous.

Penelope kept on their trail. When Penelope saw that they were going into Maison de Beauchene, she used her key to go in through the front door. She figured she'd spy on their little impromptu date night. Besides, Penelope was hoping to get some ammunition to use against her so-called friend, or at least get a better idea of what was going on. If she couldn't join them, she may as well try to beat them. That was her philosophy at least.

Inside, Philippe turned on the lights. "Do you eat snails?"

"I've never eaten them," Gianna admitted. "But I'm always up to try anything once."

"That's my kind of girl!"

"I don't know if they have these types of shows on French networks, but there's one show on Food Network I think you would like. The host travels around the world trying local flavors of remote villages."

"Well, I heard that in the US, some people eat fried cow brain sandwiches."

Penelope almost laughed out loud at Philippe's comment. *Ugh, what a moron!* He was trying entirely too hard to impress this generic woman. *Gianna is nothing special.* Penelope wanted to scream, but she bit her cheek to avoid uttering a word.

"Some people do," Gianna said. "It's popular in the central part of the country. Well, it was until mad cow disease broke out. I've never had an appetite for that one. But I do I love how integrated food and culture are. Like in Iceland, there's fermented shark. Tuna eyeballs in Japan, caterpillars in Africa, the list goes on."

Philippe looked impressed. "You would try those things?"

"I'll try anything once." That came across more suggestively than Gianna meant it too.

"That's my kind of girl." He winked at her. "I love getting creative in the kitchen. People experience so many life moments through food. It's an art that many people don't get." Philippe pulled ingredients out of the fridge.

"So what's for second dinner tonight, Chef Deneuve? I'm going to guess snails."

"Your guess would be correct. How does *cargolade* sound?"

"Like I said, I'll try anything once, but what is it?" she asked.

"It is a Catalan dish where snails are roasted in their shells with salt and pepper, some butter or lard, and just a few hints or sprinkles of spice. I'll make a simple aioli and serve it with wine."

"That definitely sounds interesting."

Philippe sensed her hesitation. "You'll like it."

He grabbed a bottle of wine and popped out the cork. He poured her a glass, but she didn't take a sip. She set the glass down beside her. Her stomach rumbled once more. Philippe grabbed a baguette and sliced it. He toasted it then added some butter, garlic spices, and parsley.

"Here you go." He handed the toast to Gianna.

She took a bite, and Philippe got back to work. Gianna sat on the counter and watched him, seeming amazed by his talent. He lit the wood-fired stove, and as it heated up, he placed the snails on a grid. He explained that they "bled" while cooking over an open-wood fire.

"Poor snails," Gianna remarked.

"Never get attached to dinner," he joked, stealing one of the pieces of toast off her plate.

Penelope smacked her head on the table she was hiding under. Oh no. She was positive that she would get caught. Her stupid plan was going to backfire like an old car, and she'd get fired! *Why do I do these types of thing to myself?*

Philippe and Gianna exchanged glances.

"What was that?" she whispered.

Philippe played the role of the calm protector. "I'll go check. Stay here."

He walked into the dining room but saw nothing and heard nothing. Outside, it looked as though a passerby had dropped a few boxes. He went back to the kitchen and found Gianna with a scared expression, holding a kitchen knife.

Philippe laughed and told her what he'd seen. "Everything is fine."

"If you say so." She placed the knife back in the knife block and ate another piece of bread.

Philippe checked the snails. "Almost done."

He prepped the aioli. He pulled the grid out of the wood-fired oven, plated the snails, and joined Gianna on the counter.

"I want to keep the lights off in the dining room so we don't attract any customers."

"There's no place I would rather be than in the kitchen," she said. "All right, master cook, let's see how well you did on this *caraolade*."

"Caraloade." He proceeded to demonstrate how the dish was eaten.

She picked up a shell and did exactly what he did.

"What's the verdict, judge?" he teased, although based on her eyes closing and her head whipping back, he guessed it was a winner.

"I like your food," she said, grinning like the Cheshire cat.

"And I like you." He had been flirting heavily with her all night, and she hadn't seemed to mind.

"What about Penelope?" Gianna asked.

"Penelope? What about her?"

"Aren't you two an item? A thing?" She gave him a look as if to say *obviously*.

Philippe laughed out loud and slapped his knee. "Penelope and me? Are you crazy? I love that girl, but she's like a sister!" He laughed again.

Gianna grew silent.

"Does this mean you'll flirt back now?" he asked with a wickedly charming smile.

"Flirt back? Does that mean you've been flirting with me?"

He bumped his shoulder into hers. "Of course it does. You're beautiful and incredible and sweet and friendly."

She smiled. "This isn't very professional of either of us, is it?"

"Nope." He thought his potential future boss had an incredible sense of humor. He was completely and totally enraptured by her easy, down-to-earth nature. *What would it be like to work beside this goddess?* He couldn't seem to shake the question, and he wasn't sure that he wanted to.

"On the topic of professional endeavors, after I talked to Penelope for the first time, when I stopped in Maison de Beauchene the other day, she mentioned how close you were with your family."

"That wouldn't hold me back..." Philippe interjected, hoping that Gianna wasn't withdrawing her offer.

"No, no, wait. Just shhh!" She held her finger up to her mouth, indicating for him to be quiet. "I have an idea. I'm thinking that there could be two Chic, Mais Oui! restaurants. One would be in Los Angeles, and the second would be right here in Paris. You would control the menu, and I would likely use your menu for the American restaurant as well, just making changes for seasonal ingredients and what we can get fresh." She paused to take a breath.

"Would you be in America or France?" he asked.

"Mostly Los Angeles. I would stay out of your way, and you would be able to stay to close to your family. Double the start-up capital but double the income! I think it would be alluring to tell guests that people across the Atlantic are sitting in the same concept."

Philippe thought it wasn't a bad idea, but his heart dropped like limp parsley at the thought of not working alongside Gianna.

In her hiding spot, Penelope heard it all, and she hated this idea! If he left Maison de Beauchene but stayed in Paris to open a newer upscale restaurant, that just meant more competition. *Why was nothing ever easy?*

Philippe and Gianna ate and talked more about the concept, throwing out ideas like Philippe's black, red, and white cinema theme. They talked about having an LA theme in Paris and a Parisian theme in LA. They talked about menu ideas, and Gianna got excited over his delectable descriptions of future menu items. The more they talked, the more Philippe was ready to make the change.

"Hey, do you want dessert?" he asked.

"I'd love some."

"Let's see." He opened the freezer. Their desserts were made fresh on the premises every day, but they usually had ice cream in the freezer. "All right, I can't offer you anything too fancy. How about ice cream?"

"I love ice cream."

Her excited expression made Philippe want to skip ice cream and kiss her for dessert. "Raspberry pistachio, coconut mango, or chocolate with cocoa nibs?"

"How much of a glutton would I be if I asked for a sample of each of them?"

"I like the way you think." Philippe grabbed one bowl and scooped the homemade flavors into it. He grabbed two spoons.

She eyed the bowl. "Oh my gosh! I can't eat all that. Are you not eating?"

"I thought we could share." He waved the two spoons. "Is that okay?"

"Sure."

Philippe set the bowl on the stainless steel counter and handed Gianna a spoon.

She dipped the spoon in the bowl, and when the creamy dessert touched her lips, she threw her head back and sighed. "Mmmm! This is the best stuff I've ever had in my life. Seriously."

She tried a different flavor, and Philippe watched her, bewitched by everything about her.

Penelope had grown irate in her hiding spot. Philippe couldn't get the job and the girl, leaving her with nothing. It was time for her to take matters into her own hands. *I have the perfect idea to ruin Philippe's perfect plan.* An evil laugh played in her head as she watched the lovebirds finish their ice cream with ooey-gooey love-struck faces.

CHAPTER ELEVEN

The next morning at work, Arnauld paced frantically in the kitchen. *Where is it? Where is it? Where could it possibly be? My recipe!*

He kept it in exactly the same place, always. The *coup de grace* of his restaurant had disappeared from his office. No one, *no one* made *coq au vin* like Arnauld. His special spice ratios and secret ingredient made it the crème de la crème of all the coq au vin in Paris, perhaps even in France. He was famous for that recipe. He knew every ingredient and instruction by heart, but his panic was because of the fact that someone else had it. The only question was, who?

It was *his* recipe and his recipe alone. In fact, no one else in his kitchen was even allowed to make it. Magazine critics raved over it, and restaurant patrons couldn't get enough. Loyal diners came in weekly for his chicken with wine sauce. Arnauld must find the recipe, even if he had to die trying.

Neither Penelope nor Philippe had ever seen Arnauld in such a state of paranoia.

"Philippe! Penelope!" He said in a stupor, "I don't think either of you did this, but I'm going to interview everyone here to see if we can find any common steps. We're going to trace steps and solve this mystery. Penelope, get started on peeling, deveining, and washing the shrimp for tonight's cognac shrimp with lemon buerre. Philippe, in my office now!"

Philippe trudged behind Arnauld into the tiny office just off the kitchen. He felt incredibly guilty about bringing Gianna there the night before. They certainly hadn't touched the recipe, but he couldn't help feeling as though his breaking and entering was worse than it had been.

"Sit, sit!" Arnauld demanded.

Once Philippe sat on the tall stool across from the desk covered with cookbooks and piles of notes, Arnauld instructed him to tell him about his past week.

"Have you seen anything unusual? Have you noticed any of the waiters or waitresses or hostesses or food vendors back here? You know the rules. My office is off limits," Arnauld said.

"I haven't noticed anything, not even last night."

Arnauld's eyes became as big as flying saucers. "What do you mean not even last night? Monday is your night off. Hell, the whole restaurant is closed."

No! Philippe hadn't meant to unwittingly implicate himself. Now he had no choice but to confess his late-night shenanigans with Gianna. "I promise you that I did not touch your recipe. I know how much it means to you, how much you mean to me."

Arnauld saw right through his flattery. "Boy, don't you mess with me. Answer the question, yes or no. Were you here last night?"

Arnauld's face reddened. Philippe hated seeing him like this. Arnauld was rarely this angry. The only time he had come close was when a newspaper writer from Spain had written that Arnauld's food was "above average but nothing extraordinary." After Arnauld had read that, he was convinced that something had gone wrong. He retraced every single step to figure out exactly which night that reviewer had dined at Maison de Beauchene, which person had waited on him, and practically tortured the waitress until she remembered every detail of what the man ate.

It turned out the averageness came not from the food but from the wine pairing. Arnauld then took the liberty of doing something wholly inappropriate. He tracked down the reviewer at his house in a different country and asked him to try the same dish he had ordered with a Sauvignon Blanc wine. The guy thought that Arnauld had lost his mind but obliged. The following issue of the paper including a new review stating Arnauld was the best of the best.

The point was, Arnauld dug for answers, and more importantly, Arnauld always found the answers he was looking for. Philippe figured that he may as well confess. He had already incriminated himself, but he was innocent of stealing the recipe. Innocent until proven guilty, right? He hoped so at least. He would never, ever betray Arnauld's trust. He was where he was because of Arnauld.

"Did you take it? The recipe?" Arnauld asked.

"I did not. However, you should know that I came into the restaurant last night with a girl. I was trying to impress her. I shouldn't have, but I didn't see anything strange or different."

"I don't believe you!" Arnauld roared.

"Wait? What?" Philippe seemed dumbfounded by his boss's response.

"You heard me. You know the rules. No one is in my kitchen unless they're getting paid and under my watch. You are my assistant. I own this place. How dare you break the rules!"

"Arnauld, I'm sorry. It was stupid. I was foolish."

"Stupid and foolish? Those are things that should get you arrested. I should call the police and file a report on you right this minute! You're a burglar! Did you cook with my food? Use my dishes? Use my cleaning supplies? This is unacceptable. I'm calling the authorities right now." There was a look of calmness on his face, although Arnauld was acting like an insane person.

"Please, Arnauld, no. I-I can pay you back for the food costs. I understand you're mad, but you have to believe me. I know nothing about the missing recipe. Please!"

"I don't believe you," he said. "I'm sorry, Philippe, but you broke into my restaurant."

"I have a key! It's not breaking and entering if you have a key." Philippe's weak testimony did not help his case.

"It is if you know you're not supposed to be somewhere. How can I trust you? You have destroyed my trust in you and my faith that you are capable of running this place. You took the recipe, didn't you? I want my coq au vin recipe back. You have until the end of the night to get it to me, or I am calling the cops. You are excused." Arnauld pointed at the door.

"Just so you know, I know absolutely nothing about the recipe going missing. I hope you will choose to believe me." Philippe walked out when Arnauld gave him no response.

"Penelope, get in here!" Arnauld screamed.

Penelope appeared at the doorway with lightning speed. "Yes, sir."

"Close the door," Arnauld barked.

When Penelope sat across from Arnauld, her voice was drenched in sweetness. "We'll find this missing recipe. I'll make it my personal mission."

"Trace your steps, Solomon!"

"Before I do that, there's something I think you should know. It's about Philippe."

Penelope's grim face made Arnauld lean in closer. "Go on."

"That girl, Gianna, that he was with last night? She's starting a restaurant in America. She wants Philippe to come work for her."

Arnauld felt anger boiling in his face, as if he wasn't angry enough already. "The pretty one? He was talking about her the other day."

"She isn't that pretty."

Arnauld ignored her comment. Either Philippe or the American had his property, his beloved, famous coq au vin recipe. "Go grab Philippe. I need to talk to him one more time."

"Yes, sir!" Penelope scattered from the office

Philippe returned to the office and faced Arnauld. "I swear that I did not take your recipe."

"I'm giving you one chance, Deneuve. One chance, and only one chance! Did you take my recipe?" Arnauld slammed his hand on the desk. "Did you take it?"

Philippe looked him directly in the eye. "I did not take your recipe. I would never do that to you."

"You must be a pathological liar. I don't believe you. I gave you the chance to come clean, but you didn't. If you had come clean, I would have considered forgiveness. We've all made mistakes, and I'm a good guy here. You leave me no choice. Philippe Deneuve, you are fired as of immediately."

"You're firing me for something I didn't do?" Philippe sounded dumbfounded.

"Penelope told me that you're thinking about going to that girl's restaurant, and now you bring her here? When you knew you shouldn't? You have broken and entered, and you have stolen. Get out of my sight. I'm going to count to three, and if you haven't gotten out of here, I'm going to have you arrested! One..." Arnauld held up a finger and picked up the phone.

Philippe tried to say something, but Arnauld just counted to two. Before he could get to three, Philippe slammed the office door behind him.

As he stormed toward the back entrance of the restaurant, he thought about Gianna. Was there any way she could have been so desperate for Chic, Mais Oui! to succeed that she would steal? Had she come to Maison de Beauchene and gone through Philippe just to execute her coy plot? It seemed so unlike her, but the timing was awfully uncanny.

How will I dig myself out of this mess? Philippe couldn't pinpoint the moment that everything had started spiraling out of control, but Gianna seemed to be a common thread in all of his problems from the past few days.

Right before he reached the door, he heard Arnauld's voice boom, "Don't let him leave!"

Several co-workers, Penelope included, apprehended Philippe. Not long after, two police officers showed up.

"Philippe Deneuve? You are under arrest for one account of breaking and entering and one account of theft."

The next two days flashed by in a blurry haze for Philippe. He was locked up in jail, where he languished for forty-eight helpless hours. Things only got worse when the newspapers picked up on the scandal, and Philippe's name was tarnished.

CHAPTER TWELVE

A handsome, clean-cut man in an Armani suit wrote a check. He handed it to the man behind the glass. The man gave him a form to sign, and he did so before sitting in one of the cold steel chairs in the small waiting area. He pulled out his cell phone.

"No cell phones, sir. Please put it away."

Startled, the guy looked up and saw a menacing guard pointing at the wall behind him. A sign clearly said, "No cell phones or electronics in the waiting room."

"Sorry." He slid the phone back into his pocket. He sat there for what felt like an eternity, but it was likely around fifteen minutes.

Finally, he heard the employee behind the glass calling out to the back. "Bring out Deneuve, Philippe, number 15784."

He waited about five more minutes and almost fell asleep sitting up until he heard a loud noise that made him jump.

Beeeeep!

The guard pressed a button, and the buzzer indicated that the door from the jail had been unlocked. Philippe was free at last. The guards released Philippe, and he signed some paperwork.

Philippe was wearing the same clothes he had been arrested in, and he hadn't shaved, but he had never looked so happy to see his older brother Luc.

Once Philippe was free to go, Luc had many questions. "What happened? You were in jail. Your name is all over the news!"

"Listen, I'm so, so grateful and appreciative that you came down here to bail me out of this place, but right now, I've got to find someone," Philippe said.

"You have a number. You have a permanent record. Mom and Dad are worried sick. If they weren't on vacation, they would be here. I have to fill them in. You have to give me something."

"Okay, this was all a big misunderstanding. And thanks for pointing out that I have a record now. Next time I go to jail, I'll call someone else to bail me out."

"I can't believe it. The easygoing, agreeable Philippe Deneuve spent two days in jail. Never did I think this would happen. Out of anyone in the family, you? Just tell me one thing, did you take the recipe? The famous recipe?"

"Do you think I took it?" Philippe asked his brother.

"No."

"Good answer. It was a misunderstanding. Although..." Philippe paused. "Can you give me a ride over to the Four Seasons? I really need to find Gianna."

Philippe didn't want to be in that prison cell for another second. It certainly wasn't a place he wanted to return to.

Luc had taken their parents' car. On the way to the hotel, Philippe told Luc all about his first, and, he hoped, last, prison experience. The food had been inedible. It tasted like the cheapest type of frozen dinners: mystery meat, puke-colored peas, and mashed potatoes that had probably been made a week earlier. He also learned that prison was incredibly boring.

Luc told him all about the headlines, which was how he'd even known that his brother had been arrested. Philippe was being portrayed as a wannabe chef and a thief.

"All I know is I'm now in the middle of a stupid court case," Philippe said. "They're even going to put me on trial. This is all a bunch of crap. Why is this happening?"

"Things were going too well for you. You know that whatever things are too good, karma has to throw you a curve ball. You're just getting all of your bad crap out of the way now." Luc honked to make a slow-poke driver go faster.

"If you say so, buddy. I think someone is out to get me. I just haven't figured out who or why. But someone is most definitely ruining my life on purpose." Philippe leaned back in the seat.

"We're being a little dramatic there, aren't we, bro?"

When they finally pulled onto the side street leading to the hotel, Philippe thanked Luc a final time and rushed inside. He looked like a hooligan in his dirty clothes, but he couldn't waste a second. He had to find Gianna. He got to the hotel's check-in desk, out of breath.

The clerk glanced at him incredulously. "May I help you?"

"Yes! I'm looking for Gianna Delano."

He heard the *click, click, clack* as the man typed in some information.

"I am sorry, sir. No one by that name is currently staying here. Is there anything else I can help you with?" The man looked professional yet irritated. His expression said, *Why is this hooligan still standing in front of me?*

"Did she leave a note? A message? Did she leave anything at for me? My name is Philippe. Philippe Deneuve."

"Let me check, sir."

The desk attendant was clearly ready for him to leave, but Philippe had to exhaust all possible options.

The lady at the next desk to him, "Philippe Deneuve? The chef? I read about you this morning!"

"Don't believe everything you read," Philippe muttered.

The man helping him returned and shook her head. "I'm sorry—I don't have anything for you. Now, is there anything else I can assist you with?"

"That's all. Thanks for your help." Philippe hung his head in disbelief and defeat.

Where had Gianna gone? Why did she leave? He had checked his email on Luc's phone since he'd been released. He had checked his voicemail. He'd had to shuffle through endless messages from his worried mom, angry father, friends, brothers, sisters, and co-workers. There were even a few media emails requesting interviews about the scandal, but there had been nothing from Gianna.

He was supposed to meet her at one of his favorite bistros in Paris to finalize the job details, but he had been stuck in jail with no way to get in touch with her. She probably he thought he had blown her off, and he hated thinking that he'd disappointed her. However, as soon as she saw the headlines, there was no way she would still want him opening up a Parisian restaurant.

Chic, Mais Oui! would be a laughingstock of the food world if he were involved in it. He could just envision the headlines: Thieving Chef Starts New Restaurant! Coq Au Vin Copycat at Chic, Mais Oui!

He groaned as he walked back to his place. Could this get any worse?

***

Across town, Gianna boarded her flight and got settled in for take-off.

"Ladies and gentlemen, the captain has turned on the Fasten Seat Belt sign. If you haven't already done so, please stow your carry-on luggage underneath the seat in front of you or in an overhead bin. Please take your seat and fasten your seat belt. Also make sure your seat back and folding trays are in their fully upright position."

The flight attendant made the speech Gianna had heard a million times. She tried not to focus on the fact that the flight attendant was male—she was so used to seeing female attendants. *Don't be sexist.* She closed her eyes and revisited the events of the past couple of days.

After the bizarre night that ended with a semi-date in the kitchen at Maison de Beauchene, Philippe had walked Gianna back to her hotel. She was positive he was going to kiss her, and she wanted him to kiss her. Heck, she even thought about kissing him! They'd definitely shared a moment when the lines of professional and romantic were blurred. She knew it, and she was pretty sure he knew it too.

The jet's engines revved, and she felt the aircraft power up.

While they lingered outside the hotel, Gianna and Philippe had made plans to finalize the job details. They were supposed to meet at a little bistro that Philippe raved about with his devilishly handsome grin. The lunch outing was for the following day.

The plane taxied to the runway.

Gianna had dressed with her impeccable style but with less formality. She wore skinny jeans tucked into tall boots and a sweater pulled over a button-up shirt. Her hair was fixed Audrey Hepburn-style in a high ponytail with sunglasses in lieu of a tiara. She showed up right on time—a few minutes early, actually. Her anticipation of seeing Philippe again was overwhelming, and she had flutters in her stomach. She sat at a table by the window, and she waited. And waited and waited and waited. After the waitress had come by three times, Gianna ordered a soup and salad combination.

Philippe never came. As she waited for him, she came to the realization that Philippe Deneuve was a fickle flirt. He had led her on and changed his mind. Gianna must have completely misjudged their date, and that was why he hadn't put the moves on her.

How foolish could I be? She wondered as she felt her body ascend, heading back to her homeland. She'd fly into New York City and from New York back to Los Angeles. With every mile that passed, Gianna tried to push Philippe further and further out of her mind.

More than the heartbreak, Gianna wanted to know why he hadn't had the decency to just reject the job offer. An email or a text message would have been fine, but no, he'd completely blown her off. Gianna couldn't help but feel relief in addition to her other emotions. She couldn't have someone that fickle in her restaurant.

Bump! Bump! Bump!

The seat belt sign flashed on as the aircraft hit a turbulent patch of air.

***

Back in LA, Gianna felt as though she'd wasted so much time in Paris, and she regretted the entire trip. If Philippe had kissed her, the trip would have been worth it. She would have taken a rocket ship or a space shuttle all the way to the moon or a different galaxy just to have one kiss from Philippe Deneuve. But, no, she'd been rejected not once but twice.

She was now more than anxious to get hit the ground running. Chic, Mais Oui! was her baby, and she now had even less time to make her place perfect. She couldn't have a restaurant without a five-star chef, so she started sorting through her email. She made a file with all of the resumes she'd received from potential chefs. Gianna would assemble a list from the stack and start making calls. She figured if she worked fast, she would still have time to make her soft opening.

Gianna clicked on the first resume in the stack. Clyde Oddwaters had been a chef in a buffet-style restaurant. It looked as though he had never been to culinary school. He called himself the Master of the Meatball. This Master of the Meatball was going into the never pile.

Next up, Olivia Gilmore. She seemed like a potential. She had graduated from Johnson and Wales, worked on an organic farm, and toured the world after college, living in hostels and cooking alongside local friends. *Olivia Gilmore, you go in the maybe pile.*

Gianna felt more hopeful as she learned about Ethan Danes. He had graduated at the top of his class from a small culinary school. She loved the sample menu that he'd attached. It sounded as though he was right in line with her modern French vision, and he spoke fluent French. That was a huge bonus. *Ethan Danes? You also go into the maybe pile.*

CHAPTER THIRTEEN

After his unsuccessful attempt at finding Gianna, Philippe attended to his second order of business—a trip to see Arnauld. Philippe still had his key to the restaurant, so he let himself in through the employee entrance.

Facing Arnauld again was the absolute last thing that Philippe wanted to do. Philippe had never a violent person, but he would love nothing more than to punch Arnauld square between the eyes.

When Philippe walked into Arnauld's office, Arnauld looked shocked to see him. "Deneuve? What are you doing here? I figured you would be making coq au vin with the American by now."

"No, I just got out of my vacation at prison, thanks to you. I came to return my key and tell you for the last time that I didn't take your stupid recipe."

"That is blasphemous. Don't you dare call my recipe stupid! I can call you stupid because you are, but that recipe is the best in the world."

"Whatever. Here's your key." It took Philippe a minute to get the key off the ring, but when he did, he firmly placed it on the desk. "You're going to feel like an imbecile when you find the recipe and realize that you have slandered my name."

"We'll see about that. Get out. You're trespassing. I'll call the police."

"I'll leave soon. Look, I just wanted to drop this off and see if you have changed your mind. Can you at least drop the court trial?" Philippe pleaded.

"Drop the court trial? Absolutely not! You did the crime, you pay the time."

"Thanks for helping me launch my career then completely destroying it." Philippe accepted that their conversation was getting him nowhere. When he turned around for his walk of innocent shame, he felt more depressed than he'd ever felt.

"Oh, and try not take anything else on your way out," Arnauld said. "See you in court."

Philippe couldn't believe that this whole debacle had ended up with prison and a court trial. It was all over a recipe, a piece of paper or, as Arnauld called it, "intellectual property."

Philippe had to appear before a court of law and defend his innocence. He might be out on bail, but this would ruin his life beyond prison. No job and a criminal. *How did I get here?*

As he closed the door to Maison de Beauchene, a piece of him withered and died. He had poured his heart and soul into that place. He'd spent countless nights and weekend and mornings and afternoons making sure the place was perfect. It was more than a job, more than a career. This place was a passion. Just like a bandage being ripped off, the position had been ripped off of him. It was heartbreaking.

He put his hands in his back pockets, and he walked about a block before he heard someone yelling his name.

"Philippe! Stop! Philippe! Philippe!"

He turned around and saw Penelope. Aside from Arnauld, she was the last person he wanted to see, but he stopped and waited for her to catch up.

"What do you want?"

"Wait? You're mad at me?" Penelope blinked innocently. "It's not my fault Arnauld promoted me to the interim sous-chef."

"I didn't know that part, but really, Penelope? You threw me under a bus. You told him that Gianna was with me at Maison de Beauchene. How did you know that? I certainly never told you. And why in the world would you say something to Arnauld? You messed me up. I want you out of my life."

Penelope froze. "I was out for a walk and saw you two go into the restaurant."

"We came in through the back entrance."

"I saw you guys walk down the side street. I was going to come over and apologize, but you two looked so sweet and cozy together. I'm sorry. You saw what kind of a rage Arnauld was in the other day. He was asking so many questions, and it just slipped out. It wasn't intentional."

Philippe could understand that. Arnauld had been a crazy person that day. He let out a sigh as he shook his head. "Fine." He held up his hands in surrender.

"I need to get back to work, but whatever you need, I'm here for you. I can write you a letter of recommendation, be a reference. You'll get through this, I just know it." She squeezed his hand.

"Thanks. Oh, do you know where Gianna is? She checked out of her hotel, and I haven't seen her. Did she stop by the restaurant looking for me? Anything?"

"I haven't seen her, but I knew something seemed off about her. I'm sorry she left without a word. It was probably for the best, but I know how much you like her."

"Thanks. This just sucks so much, all of it," Philippe said.

"Chin up, pal. If this is rock bottom, things can only go up from here." She gave him a half-smile before strolling back to work.

He had told her that exact same phrase when she'd hit rock bottom a few years earlier. He had been there for her, and he was hoping she'd be there for him now.

"Oh, Philippe?" Penelope turned back around. "Is there any chance that Gianna took the recipe? When she was with you that night at the restaurant?"

"I've thought about it, but there's no way. She was with me the entire time, I think."

"Well, just a thought. You should try to find her." She waved before leaving Philippe alone on the street.

Penelope's idea wasn't lost on him. He had questioned the same thing. Had Gianna taken the recipe? There was only one way to find out. Penelope was wrong most of the time, but this time she seemed to be his voice of reason.

He called the airlines and booked a standby ticket, the cheapest ticket he could get. In less than a day, he would be in the United States and trying to find his girl. He may have to play detective, but he was determined. He wasn't supposed to go far due to the pending court case, but he knew it would be at least two weeks before his case made the docket. He'd only be gone a few days and no one would notice. Everything he had ever worked for was on the line. Gianna might be able to redeem him, and that was worth his savings.

On the morning of his flight, he texted Penelope before he took a taxi to the airport:

Hey Penelope! Thanks for the advice the other day. I'm flying to LA to try to find Gianna. I think you're right. If she has the recipe, my name will be cleared. Thanks again for the encouragement and we will talk soon. Your friend, Philippe

***

What a night. Penelope was exhausted and yawned. The shift had been rough without Philippe by her side. She'd taken over his responsibilities, and her assistant just wasn't as fast or as good as Philippe. The girl didn't tell jokes and was a total bore. Not to mention three people had sent food back to the kitchen. One person's meat was undercooked, and Penelope was shocked to see how pink the chicken was in the middle. One person had specks of dirt in their salad, and the other person's food was too cold.

She has a new appreciation for Philippe. But instead of regretting her sabotage plan, she used it as fuel to be better, quicker, and faster. She must prove to Arnauld that she was better, that she was the best. She took out her phone to check it before going to bed. Philippe had texted her. Quickly, she read it.

Ha! He did it. He took my advice! She laughed. Her goal of solidifying her position at Maison de Beauchene was one stop closer to becoming a reality.

As Penelope unlocked the door to her apartment and changed out of her dirty chef's uniform, her mind raced. She shouldn't be doing this to Philippe. She knew it was messed up. She recalled how ragged and tired her friend had looked when she last saw him, and she felt genuine remorse, but she was too far into this mess to correct it. Her booty was on the line, and she needed this job. Philippe was charming, and Penelope knew that people didn't like her.

Penelope heard people at work whispering and talking about her all the time. She had tried so hard to get ahead in life, but she never seemed to fit in. She tried to speak in a sophisticated fashion, but sometimes her message got jumbled. She'd use big words in a sentence but use them in the wrong context. People seemed to get angry at her no matter what she said anyway.

Her clothes weren't good enough, and she was no model. If people found out about her mother and father, then they would think she was worthless, even though she had risen above her ramshackle of an upbringing. Growing up, she'd told herself that she wasn't worth their effort. Nobody wanted her. A dozen years later, she still had those very same thoughts.

Philippe didn't want her either. But maybe her revenge on Philippe wasn't just about him. Maybe this was about every single person who had wronged her, who didn't believe her, or who made fun of her. Philippe was the one who gave her a chance, so he was the only one she knew to sabotage. He was her puppet, and she was finally the puppeteer. For the first time in her life, Penelope was in control, and nobody could take that away from her. Her next move was simple. She just needed to alert the authorities of Philippe's escape, but she had one thing to take care of first.

"I'm sorry, Philippe," she whispered.

CHAPTER FOURTEEN

Once his plane landed in Los Angeles, Philippe knew that the first place to check for Gianna was Chic, Mais Oui! He remembered she had said it was off of the famous Rodeo Drive, so he had the taxi driver drop him off near the midpoint of the road, and he carried his luggage with him like a vagabond. Since the trip was supposed to be a short one, he had only brought his carry-on.

He walked down the street and recognized one that sounded familiar, the address of Chic, Mais Oui! so he turned down it. It was blazing hot outside and he desperately wanted a glass of water, but he suppressed the need in order to continue his hunt. Fortunately, the street he was on was more shaded than Rodeo Drive. He felt like a leprechaun who had found his pot of gold when he saw the sign for Chic, Mais Oui! The windows had signs announcing that the restaurant was "coming soon." They also showed the address of the boutique eatery's website.

The place looked incredible even though it was still a work in progress. *You've done well, Gianna.* He caught his breath, and trying to clean himself up, he wiped the sweat off his face and tussled his curly hair. He gave his head a quick shake. *It is what it is.* He had plane hair, and he probably smelled, but there was nothing to do about it now.

Of course Philippe was upset that Giana had just disappeared, but she probably thought he had stood her up. All Philippe knew was that he desperately wanted to clear things up with his beautiful American friend.

Here goes nothing. He quietly knocked on the door, not wanting to startle her too much. He waited a minute but didn't hear anything at all. He knocked again with a little more force.

He heard footsteps on the other side of the wall, then a woman called, "Who is it?"

The adorable voice made Philippe grin from ear to ear. She was there. He would recognize

Gianna's voice anywhere. "Gianna! It's Philippe. Philippe Deneuve."

He heard the lock twist, and she opened the door. Philippe was greeted with a look of pure shock. Gianna looked as if she was seeing a ghost.

"Hi," he said.

She was speechless at first. "What are you doing here?"

"I had to see you. I had to find you. I'm so sorry about everything."

Gianna held her finger up to her mouth, as if to say "Be quiet," and held the door open so that he could come in. "I'm doing a closed tasting from the list of resumes I gathered. I still need to find a chef."

There was an awkward silence between them after those last words rolled off her tongue. Still, Philippe thought his surprise visit was off to a good start so far. Maybe there was hope. Maybe, just maybe, this whole mess could be salvaged.

Once inside the restaurant, his eyes wandered everywhere. The restaurant was immaculate. Most of the construction had been completed, and Chic, Mais Oui! was absolutely stunning. She had taken Philippe's idea for upscale elegance. The floors were a deep, dark hardwood. The tabletops each had a tall, skinny square vase that would be filled with even taller arrangements of flowers. Square, modern, chunky lights dangled from the wood beams in the ceiling. The bar was stocked with a cool, multi-level look to it, and one wall had tea lights floating on it.

"Gianna, this place is amazing," he said.

"Looks only get you so far. Once I find my chef, I'll relax. This is so stressful that I'm wondering what I was thinking. What have I gotten myself into?"

Philippe hoped he could help her, but before he could even think about the chef job, he needed to talk to her about the recipe. He was about to start that tough conversation when she spoke.

"Hey, I need to try out these dishes while they're still warm. Do you want to come back to the kitchen and help me judge them? Are you hungry after your plane ride?"

"I could eat. I wonder if it's as good as my food. We'll see what kind of dishes these French chef impersonators are making," he teased.

Seeing how tense she was, he didn't want to talk about the recipe thieving just yet. All the way to Los Angeles, he had convinced himself that Gianna had taken it and used him. He made up a whole elaborate story of how she'd picked him out of the crowd and feigned attraction to lure him in just to ruin his life. The minute he saw her again, he felt silly for thinking that she was guilty.

She simply looked like a hard-working, disheveled, albeit gorgeous person trying to start a restaurant. Philippe was so used to seeing her impeccably dressed, but today, Gianna was wearing yoga pants and a light-weight, purple zip-up jacket. He thought she was magnificent, even in grungier clothes. He felt foolish for thinking that she was the recipe thief, but he reminded himself that she could still be fooling him.

Back in the kitchen, he noticed that everything was brand-spanking new: the stoves, the ovens, the pots, and the pans. He envied the chef who got to help start this establishment from the ground up. Chic, Mais Oui! had all the makings of a successful restaurant: beautiful atmosphere, devoted owner, clean kitchen, and an incredible location. All that was missing was the chef.

On one of the stainless steel counters were samples of many dishes, broken into several rows.

"I had the potential chefs bring over a trio of mini-dishes. I'm tasting and judging them.

Here, grab a fork!" She pulled one out of the silverware caddy for each other.

It took him right back to their quasi-date, the night before everything fell apart. Gianna had a clipboard and made notes as she tried the different dishes. In true food-judge fashion, she took small bites. If a judge took too many bites, they could become biased. The rule was one bite. Well, that was Gianna's rule anyway.

She took a good look at Philippe. He was as handsome as always, but he looked tired, stressed out even. But that was probably because of the long flight.

At the top of the list, she penciled in Philippe's name. She really hoped that he had flown to LA and found her to say that he had reconsidered. He might be fickle in love, but the man was loyal to his job, and he could cook.

Based on the samples, Gianna was able to narrow her list down to three PCs, or potential chefs. Four, if she included Philippe. Although she was more than happy he was there, she couldn't help feeling as if something was off about him. She guessed it was just her personal feeling about being stood-up and rejected, but some of those feelings had melted off and evaporated.

She had thought about the handsome Philippe Deneuve every single day since she'd left France. A girl didn't have those kinds of thoughts then hold a grudge when he flew thousands of miles to see her.

Philippe lingered around Chic, Mais Oui! while she finished her day, neither of them daring to ask the question that hung in the air of why he was really there.

Finally, Gianna broke through the barrier. "So, Philippe, I'm dying to know. Why did you fly to LA?" She wiped her hands on a dishrag and propped her elbows on the counter. "Are you here about the job? You know you could have called or emailed."

"I didn't have your phone number or your email address, just the number for the hotel, which was what I used when you were in Paris." His heart beat a quicker pitter-patter, speeding up the adrenaline rushing through his veins.

"What are you talking about? I gave you both." Gianna stopped leaning on the counter and put her hands on her hips.

"No, you had my email. You were supposed to send me an email with your phone number in it, remember?" Philippe began doubting her innocence once again.

"I sent it but never got a response. Here, let me show you." She rummaged through her purse until she found her phone. She pulled up her email app then scrolled through the sent items until she found the message sent to Philippe. She handed the phone to him and did a victory dance. "See? I told you. I'm right, and you're wrong."

He joined in on her teasing game. "Nope, you're wrong."

"You're crazy. Read it. Sent at 3:47 p.m."

"You gave some other guy your phone number. Nice going, kid." He smiled as she refused to accept her defeat.

"What? No way." She stood close to him and stayed there for a moment.

Philippe took a mini-step backward and showed her the phone. "You typed my name wrong."

"I didn't!" Gianna persisted.

"It's one L and two P's, not two L's and one P."

"Oh, shoot."

He smiled at her. "I cannot believe you gave some random guy your number. If he knew how cute you are, he'd be calling you nonstop."

Her cheeks reddened, and she smiled back. "Well, I just have to keep my options open. What if Philippe with one P is cuter than you?"

"Ha, ha. You're a funny, funny girl... not."

"Philippe, what are you really doing here?" she asked.

Philippe took a couple of larger steps away from Gianna and sighed.

"Well...?" Gianna looked at him impatiently.

"You didn't read the news at all in Paris?"

"No. I read the *New York Times* at the hotel. Why, did something bad happen?"

"The morning after our night in the Maison de Beauchene kitchen, things sort of, how do I say this... blew up."

Her eyes widened. "Literally? What happened?"

"No, no, not literally. The next day, I went into the work, and my boss was pissed. I figured that he'd found out that I had brought you to the restaurant after hours, which is a big no-no in Arnauld's kitchen."

"I'm so sorry. I didn't mean to get you in trouble."

He could tell she felt bad, but he wondered if it was just a game. Was she just faking the sweet and innocent look? This was LA, and she was a model—was she also an actress? He felt as if he was on a hidden camera reality show. "No, that was only part of it. It turns out my boss's prized, famous recipe for a certain dish stolen." He didn't say that it was for coq au vin because he hoped that she may mention it and incriminate herself.

She stared at him blankly. "Okay..."

He continued. "He thinks that I stole it. The night that we were there, it went missing. Do you know anything about it? Did you see it? Did you..."

Gianna interrupted him angrily. "Wait a minute, are you saying I took it?"

"No, not at all." He paused. "Well, maybe."

Gianna grew angrier. "So you flew all the way here to accuse me of taking a stupid recipe? Wow! You are—you are a piece of work, Philippe. You stand me up and now this?"

"Please calm down. The reason I stood you up was because my boss accused me of stealing intellectual property. Penelope saw us going into the restaurant, and she told Arnauld. I just—I just had to do something." He could see Gianna was climbing down from the top of her anger mountain. He decided to drop the topic. He was pretty sure that she hadn't taken it, but she did get awfully defensive. "Look, this was stupid. I don't think you took it. I just needed to see for myself. I promise I didn't stand you up. I would never do that. Believe me?"

"Fine," she said half-heartedly.

"Since I'm here, I want to make it up to you."

"How long are you here? In Los Angeles?"

"A few days. I was hoping that you would be my tour guide. Will you show me around?"

She paused, considering it, before saying, "I'd love to."

CHAPTER FIFTEEN

"*L*et me run to my apartment and shower. Then we'll meet back–where are you staying?" Gianna asked.

He told her the hotel's street address.

"I'll pick you up in a couple hours?"

"Perfect. I need to get checked in, and a shower sounds good to me too." Philippe was almost one hundred percent positive that he believed Gianna, but he planned to watch her behavior over the next few days, just in case she was hiding something. He felt like a turkey for doing this, but his life and livelihood were on the line.

"Actually, do you want a ride?" she asked. "I'll drop you off."

"That would be great, if you don't mind."

A little while later, after she'd dropped him off and picked him back up, she asked if there was anything special he wanted to do.

"I'll be honest, I haven't actually explored much of Los Angeles. When I was here for the show, I jumped off the plane and did my work thing for the camera, then I jumped right back on a plane."

Gianna smiled. "This will be fun. I know the perfect starting point. Traffic will be awful, but we'll get there."

"Sounds good. Where are we going?" he asked.

"It's a surprise!"

The sun was still shining in the early summer evening and the humidity was low. It was the perfect opportunity for Gianna and Philippe to ride with the top down in her two-door coupe convertible.

"I figured you would have a red sports car," Philippe admitted.

"Red is too much of a cliché. I like my little silver car. Silver Sandy is her name." Gianna found a parking spot and turned to Philippe. "Welcome to the Venice Beach Boardwalk."

Philippe didn't know whether this was officially a date or just two friends hanging out, but he decided to set the tone early—by flirting heavily.

Gianna said she didn't have anything planned besides just walking around. There was so much to see at the boardwalk, including bikers, skateboarders, and Rollerbladers.

"This place is so different than what you see in Paris," Philippe exclaimed. "Everyone is so relaxed."

Gianna laughed. "I doubt anyone would wear tie-dye in Paris." They passed a hot dog vendor cart, and Gianna asked, "Do you want one?"

"Sure, I've never tried a hot dog before."

"Really? You've never had a hot dog? Then you must, right now. Let me buy you one."

"No, that's okay." He dug up his wallet but realized that in his rush, he hadn't exchanged his euros to dollars. He felt guilty for not paying, but she insisted.

The guy manning the cart asked Philippe what he wanted on his hot dog. Philippe said he'd take it however Gianna took hers.

"Everything," she said. "Ketchup, mustard, chili, pickles, and onions. With a whole bunch of napkins."

The vendor handed over their hot dogs, which were wrapped in aluminum foil. Gianna grabbed his hand and pulled him toward the pier. "Let's see if we can find a spot on the pier to eat."

As they walked along the pier, they passed a snake charmer. Gianna squeezed Philippe's hand and scooted closer to him.

"What, you don't like snakes?" he asked.

"No. I'm terrified of them."

"I won't let him get you, babe." He squeezed her hand tighter. They walked in silence, then Philippe made slithering noises, imitating the snake.

"Stop it!" She squealed with delight, which only made him laugh harder.

A couple stood up from a bench on the pier, and Gianna grabbed it for her and Philippe.

"So how do I eat this?" Philippe asked, unwrapping his hot dog dinner.

"Well, you bite into it." She watched, looking amused, as he tried it. "What do you think?"

"It's really good. Er, what exactly is in a hot dog?" He used a napkin to wipe some chili from his chin.

"You definitely do not want to know the answer to that question."

He looked concerned, but when Gianna took a bite of hers, he continued eating. After dinner, they walked along the beach. The water felt amazing, and they watched surfers on the waves and young children building castles in the sand. They took every opportunity to hold hands, bump into each other, or playfully touch.

Philippe stifled a yawn. "The time difference has gotten to me."

"Let's head back. What do you want to do tomorrow?" Gianna asked.

"I want to spend time with you. I don't care what we do."

"Sounds good to me! Oh, and Philippe?"

He turned around, thinking he might kiss her... or maybe she would kiss him. Instead, he was greeted by her devilish smile.

"I keep good on my promises. If I say I'm going to be somewhere, I'm going to be there!" she said.

"You're a funny girl, Gianna Delano."

***

The next day, Gianna showed up at Philippe's hotel, looking wildly hot and armed with an arsenal of options for him to choose from to do that day.

Since he only had forty-eight hours left in his trip, Gianna said she wanted to make sure they were perfect. "Whatever you want to do, I'm up for it."

"Okay, there is one thing. I'd love to see the big Hollywood sign. The big white letters on the side of the mountain." When Gianna laughed, he asked, "Is that stupid?"

"No, no. It's fine. Just be prepared—it's a very underwhelming experience. But you can't come to LA and not see it. Let's go!"

When they got there, Philippe asked if they could climb up and get closer.

"Only if you want to get arrested," she teased.

He winced. He had already been through that, but he didn't want to tell her about that yet.

They crammed as much as possible into the remaining time they had together. They visited Beverly Hills, Hollywood Boulevard, and the art museum, then they just drove around with the top down, soaking in the beautiful California weather.

Philippe especially loved seeing the Pacific coast. They had a beach afternoon, and Philippe couldn't stop gawking at Gianna in her bathing suit. It was a one-piece but not like the one-pieces that grandmothers wore. It was sexy and modest somehow.

While standing in the water, just letting their toes get wet as the waves crashed on them, Philippe asked her, "Can I make you dinner tonight?" He took her hand and drew her close to his chest.

A shiver ran down her spine. "At my restaurant?"

"No, in your kitchen at your apartment. I thought we could have a normal date night. Dinner and movie, that kind of thing. What do you say?"

"Let me ask you one question first." She looked down as she asked, "Do you believe me? Do you believe that I didn't take the recipe?" She felt her feet sinking into the sand, so she stepped forward, only to get splashed by a bigger wave. She jumped away, shrieking.

Philippe laughed at her dramatic overreaction. "Oh, Gianna, I never really thought you took it. Penelope filled my head with crazy ideas, and I just, I just... I panicked when everything was going so badly. I was desperate for an explanation."

"Who do you think took it?" Gianna asked.

"I honestly have no idea. I'm starting to wonder if the old bat just misplaced it." He hoped he could figure out the mystery soon. If he didn't, then this could be the last time he would see Gianna for a long, long time.

As their eyes locked, Gianna held her hand out to Philippe. "Come on, let's go throw the Frisbee before heading back."

Philippe took her hand, and she pulled him back to the warm sand. Their feet were covered with dried, caked-on sand. As he grabbed the Frisbee, a ball from nearby beach volleyball players flew past him and barely missed his head.

"Sorry, man!" the guy called, retrieving his ball.

"No problem," Philippe said courteously.

"Cool accent, bro! Where are you from? Iceland?" The guy tossed the ball between his hands.

"France."

"Awesome!" The guy went back to his game.

Gianna laughed. "Iceland? That was random."

They tossed the Frisbee back and forth until Gianna announced that she had had enough sun for the day.

***

When the taxi dropped Philippe off in front of Gianna's building, she was waiting for him in what he thought was just a simple cotton dress. Casual yet beautiful was how he would describe Gianna to anyone.

"You made it. Welcome to my home." Gianna opened her arms wide, and Philippe embraced her. They both let the embrace linger, neither wanting to let go.

A passerby called out, "Get a room!"

That made them laugh, and Gianna grabbed his hand and showed him around the apartment. As she took him on the grand tour, she pointed out the pool, a workout room, the big lobby, the mailroom, and the elevators.

"Your building is pretty nice," Philippe said as they waited for the elevator.

When the elevator dinged and the doors opened, they stepped in. Gianna hit the button for the top floor.

"You live in the penthouse suite?" Philippe asked.

"It's no big deal."

When they walked in, he said, "No big deal? This place is gorgeous!"

Gianna had decorated her house with great love. Many of the paintings were pieces she had collected from various countries. It was modern, bright, and chic with lots of whites and grays. There wasn't even a speck of dust to be found. All the windows were open, and the breeze felt rejuvenating. Philippe couldn't believe that this was Gianna's real life. It was just so *Hollywood*.

They had already bought the things they needed for dinner, and Gianna had left them in the kitchen.

"Okay, I'm cooking, so my rules." He poured her a glass of red wine. He remembered that that was her favorite wine from the night of the party. "Out of the kitchen you go."

She protested. "No, I want to hang out with you while you cook."

He handed her the glass. "Out!" He pointed for her to leave.

She sulked to the living room, where she flipped on the TV and opened a celebrity gossip magazine, which was her guilty pleasure. She tried to relax. She really enjoyed the idea of someone else cooking for her, but she was a control freak about her kitchen and having things exactly in the right place.

That was something Philippe learned as she kept going into the kitchen. Eventually, Philippe gave up and let her set the table.

"Dinner is served," Philippe said as he brought out steak with his secret meat rub, Brussels sprouts with cranberries and almonds and feta, and mascarpone cheese whipped mashed potatoes.

"I'm going to hire you to be my personal chef," she announced.

Over dinner, they talked about their childhoods and families. They shared funny bad date stories and discussed their dreams and ambitions and aspirations. They both found it so easy to talk to each other, as if they'd known each other for years.

After dinner, they carried the dishes to the sink.

"I'll clean them up tomorrow," Gianna said.

They sat on the deck overlooking Los Angeles and the pool below.

"Since I'm in charge of dessert, I think we should toast s'mores in the fire pit," she said.

She grabbed marshmallows, skewers, chocolate, and Graham crackers from inside and started the fire. As the flames heated up, so did the chemistry between Gianna and Philippe. Their touching and flirtatious banter increased as Gianna fed Philippe a bite of her s'more. Once they were full and the fire died down, they retreated into the living room.

Instead of watching a movie, they flipped through the channels. When an episode of *Ultimate Food Fighters* came on, they couldn't help watching it and reminiscing about being on the show together.

"I wanted to kiss you the minute I saw you," Philippe admitted.

"I thought you were going to kiss me that night at Maison de Beauchene," Gianna said.

"I want to kiss you now."

Without giving her a chance to say another word, Philippe leaned toward Gianna and kissed her with a fierce passion. She wrapped her arms around him and leaned in. Neither one made any move to stop it until finally Gianna pulled back from the magical kiss.

Philippe decided to be a gentleman. "I'm going to go back to my place."

She nodded, seeming to understand exactly what he was trying to say.

"Tonight was wonderful, Gianna. It was perfect."

"I completely agree."

She walked him to the door, initiated another kiss, then bid him goodnight and good-bye.

Once he was gone, she leaned against the door and thought about the wonderful days

she had shared with him and wistfully fanta-
sized about a life with the Philippe Deneuve.

CHAPTER SIXTEEN

*A*cross town, Philippe lay in his bed, trying to sleep. His hotel was nowhere near as nice Gianna's penthouse. That was what happened when one lived on his savings because he was an unemployed chef making headlines as a liar and thief. He wished he could stay with his new love.

He could see himself living with her, cooking for her, making her happy; he could see himself marrying Gianna.

Fate was beyond cruel. Philippe sighed. It was just his luck to find the girl of his dreams, only to lose her to the nightmare of the theft accusation.

It took a lot to make Philippe Deneuve want to be tied down. Like a rodeo bull, Philippe loved the game but hated being tied down. Since he couldn't sleep because of his racing mind, he decided he wanted to do something for Gianna so that she would never forget him. The thought of never seeing her again after this trip was gut-wrenching. Someone may as well have stabbed him in the heart. He totally got what Romeo had gone through.

Philippe pulled out his laptop to start recording voice memos for recipes that she could have for Chic, Mais Oui! He opened a new Excel document and created a chart, breaking it down according to category: appetizers, entrees, and desserts. He made a list of some of his favorite and the most revered dishes of his cooking career. He even included some of the dishes he had made for her, hoping they would remind her of him.

Once he had his list and the recipes typed out, he opened up a program that allowed him to record voice memos. He started with the entrée category at random, and the first voice memo he recorded was for the *branzino*. His voice cracked as he talked into the microphone as if she were truly in the room.

"Hey, Gianna, it's me, Philippe. European sea bass, also known as branzino, will make your guests weep. Make this as a special, not a regular menu item. The sea bass is expensive, but it will make loyal patrons of anyone who eats it. Keep it simple with olive oil and fresh herbs. I love using tarragon, Italian parsley, fresh chives, and coarse kosher salt. It's bliss and one of my favorite fishes. I wish I could make it for you. Think of me when you try it. I'll be thinking of you always."

The next voice memo was for his famous butternut squash and pumpkin ravioli, which he had made the night Penelope sabotaged his audition with Gianna.

"There's magic in this combination. Everyone loves ravioli, but butternut squash and pumpkin make it heavenly. It's a sweet and savory main dish that is perfect for any fall menu. It definitely has the modern look you're going for. Fresh sage that has been pan-fried is critical for a garnish. Like with all ravioli dishes served in upscale restaurants, there isn't a ton on the plate. Add a green veggic of your choice. I like broccolini with lemon and almonds. An apple-pecan harvest salad would also be a nice touch. If you make this, imagine being in Paris with me in the fall. We would have a picnic by the Eiffel Tower, and I would pack this. For us. Cheers to you, Gianna."

As he recorded memo after memo, he felt unstoppable. The last of the entrée recipes was a classic but a goodie: roasted chicken with fingerling potatoes.

"So many people request the chicken breast, but true flavor lies in the dark meat. Serve guests a blend of white and dark meat from the whole roasted chicken. Never get a chicken weighing more than four pounds—smaller is better. The same is true for asparagus—the thinner the stalks, the more flavor in the vegetable. Also, make sure your new chef can make caramelized onions. If they can't complete this task perfectly, do not hire them. This is a classic dish, but you want some of those on the menu too. Some people prefer the meat-and-potatoes type of dishes to the neo-modern stuff. This one is for them! And Gianna? You are classic. Never change who you are.

"Crème brulée needs to be on the menu at all time but only the dark chocolate. This recipe could bring world peace to even the toughest of enemies. Add in seasonal crème brulée flavors as you wish. Vanilla is great in the summer. Peppermint and/or gingerbread flavor is good for the holidays. If a guest has a bad experience, which they will—it's just a fact of the restaurant business—give them this dessert for free. It will totally negate the bad experience. Trust me! It's one of my tricks. You'll learn your own, but shortcuts are nice too. I'll make this for you one day, I promise. If you want me to, that is...

"Okay, next up is sautéed spinach. I know what you're thinking. 'Sautéed spinach? Philippe has lost his mind!' What sets apart any good restaurant is their attention to detail, down to the minute things like sautéing spinach. Make sure your chefs add a pinch of freshly grated nutmeg just before the greens start to wilt. Just try it and trust me on this, okay? I know I keep saying that. I just want everything to be perfect for this restaurant. Perfect like you..."

After he recorded the voice notes for the rest of the entrees, he moved on to desserts and finally appetizers. The memos took him all night to finish. He didn't sleep at all. Instead, he poured his heart and soul into the last-minute present for his beautiful Gianna. All in all, there were twenty-two recipes, and when Philippe saw that it was 6:48 a.m., he couldn't believe it.

"I can sleep in jail," Philippe muttered as a yawn escaped his mouth.

His heart and soul hurt in a way he had never known. This was definitely love, no other way to explain it. He had played the dating game, flirted with and gone out with many beautiful, stunning women, but not a single one had ever lit a fire in his heart like with Gianna Delano. He tried to reason with himself, creating an explanation that the whole theft, job loss, and sneaking out of the country thing had given him a heightened sense of arousal, but he knew deep down what the truth was. He, Philippe Deneuve, was madly, head over heels in love with Gianna. She could tie him down like a rodeo bull, and he would be okay with it forever and ever.

He didn't have much longer to finish his project before he had to go to the airport. He had a fleeting idea about staying there. It would be hard for the Paris police to trace his whereabouts, and he could be with Gianna. He could be an ex-pat living at large. Then he imagined the manhunt that would follow and the chaos that would surround Gianna. He couldn't do that to her, but it was an amusing thought nonetheless.

Instead, he did the gentlemanly thing. He logged into his email and crafted his message to Gianna. He felt silly typing his last name, but it seemed appropriate, adding a touch of drama to the moment. He attached all twenty-two voice memos and the document with all the recipes. Each recipe included as many tips and tricks as he could come up with. He wanted nothing more than for his girl to be successful. His girl. It was that simple. He didn't even have a second thought as he hit the send button.

Quickly, he showered, packed his small bag, and headed to the lobby to wait for the taxi he'd called. He was so thankful he'd had one more opportunity to see Gianna. Paris was supposed to be the most romantic city in the world, but it was the last place he wanted to be in at the moment.

He grabbed his stuff and stepped out when he saw the taxi pull up to the curb.

***

Gianna woke up in her giant penthouse bedroom, but when she opened her eyes, she didn't feel as though she'd slept at all. The covers were tangled, and she felt as if she'd been to war and back. Saying good-bye to Philippe the night before had been excruciating, and she wished he had stayed. She wondered what it would be like to wake up next to Philippe every day.

She groaned and covered her face with a pillow. They hardly knew each other, and she was fantasizing about marriage?

She wasn't ready to crawl out of the safe haven of her bed, so she grabbed her phone off of the nightstand and flipped through her social media accounts. After wasting time on social media, she checked her email. *I may as well get this day started.*

Her mood instantly lifted when she saw Philippe's name among the junk mail and more resumes in her inbox. She opened the email as quickly as her fingers would let her. As she read the message and saw the long list of attachments, her heart beat faster and faster.

Hello, Gianna! Good morning. I wish I could be your chef. I want to be your chef more than anything. I would stay in America and do anything I could to be with you, but since that is not a possibility, I'm giving you twenty-two of my recipes for appetizers, entrees, and desserts. Use them and always think of me when they are being cooked in your kitchen.

Look, I have to be honest with you. I'm in some serious trouble. I have told you bits of it, but it seems like such a fictional tale that I can't remember what all I have told you. I'm laying the whole story out for you now because this could be the last time we talk for a long, long while.

I have been accused of stealing my boss's coq au vin recipe, as you know. I spent time in jail, and I am awaiting a trial for stealing "intellectual property." I'm in the Parisian headlines, and of course, Arnauld fired me. When I go back, I'll likely be in prison. I just had to see you one more time. Please know that I'm innocent. You know who I am. I feel like I'm being set up, but I'm strong and will be fine, even in the face of adversity.

Gianna, you have to know that my feelings for you are real. I promise that I didn't steal that recipe, and my intentions are always honorable. I love being a chef, and I think I love you too.

Read this carefully: I want you to move forward with your life. Open your restaurant and know that I wish you the absolute best in all of your endeavors. I am so, so sorry that I won't be there to see your dream come true. I hope these recipes help with your success, although you would be fine without them.

Until we meet again!

–Philippe Deneuve

So many thoughts raced through her mind. *Poor Philippe! Wait, he loves me? Prison?!* Gianna was floored. And the recipes! She was surprised by his generous gift. She clicked on one of the voice memos at random and waited for it to download.

Hearing his voice made her heart pine for him. She knew he would never steal a recipe, or anything for that matter. She hadn't known him for long, but she could attest to his character. His arrest was so unjust! As she listened to the first memo, she couldn't believe what he had done for her. It must've taken him all night to do. He had given her the best of his recipes. With them, even if she had to hire someone new, she had the menu and recipes to get started.

Oh, Philippe! Tears burned and stung her eyes. She wanted to save him in the same way he had saved her. Tears and joy overtook her emotions, and she felt pulled in so many directions. She sat up in her bed and knew that she must go back to Paris to try to help Philippe. She had no idea what she could do to help, but she was determined to try something, anything to prove his innocence.

She thought she loved him back. She wasn't sure, but her will to fight for him seemed to be a darn good indicator of something stronger than just friendship. *Get ready, Paris, I'm coming back!* Giana would book a plane ticket as soon as possible.

CHAPTER SEVENTEEN

*P*hilippe was exhausted from working all night on the voice memos and recipes. He slept through the entire plane trip home, which was fantastic because he also got to avoid the horrible airplane food.

The pilot informed them that they were getting ready for descent, so Philippe buckled up. He'd always thought that the seat belts on planes were pointless. In the event of a plane crash, a little lap belt would help no one, yet he always obeyed and buckled it securely. A few minutes later, he felt a big bump as the plane's wheels touched the runway. They raced for a few moments before coming to a stop. The other passengers clapped. He supposed being alive was something to be grateful for, even if he was facing jail time.

He wasn't exactly sure what he planned to do for the next few days until the trial started, but he was hoping to use them make sense of the mess. But his idea of a few days of freedom came to a halt quicker than the plane.

The moment the plane stopped at the gate, the passenger door opened. Two cops barreled into the plane, handcuffs ready. And they were heading Philippe's way.

No way. They can't be for me. Philippe sighed with great resignation. *Is Arnauld's recipe really worth this much?*

The whole thing was like something out of a movie—a comedy. It could be a romantic comedy if only there would be a happy ending. At the moment, that didn't seem likely.

"Philippe Deneuve?" the taller, burlier of the two cops said briskly.

"Yes, sir, that's me." Philippe hung his head in dismay.

"You're under arrest."

How in the world had this happened? Did Gianna freak out when she read the email and alert the authorities? The only other people who knew about his quick trip were Luc and Penelope. Surely none of them would have said anything. Not that it mattered. Someone had leaked his whereabouts, but he knew he shouldn't have fled. *Me? A flight risk!* He wanted to laugh, and he did by accident.

The cops exchanged glances.

"You're under arrest for leaving the country without permission," one cop said while the other grabbed Philippe's hands and put them behind his back with force.

Philippe yelped at the force the shorter cop used. "I'm not going to put up a fight or anything, but geez, can you be a little bit more gentle?"

The taller cop showed mercy and told his colleague to ease up a bit on Philippe. The two police officers walked him out of the plane to an unmarked SUV and opened the door. Philippe got into the backseat without any struggle.

He took his seat, completely confused and bewildered. *I guess this is it. Who would have betrayed me?* He couldn't figure it out. His mind kept going back to Gianna, but he truly couldn't picture her doing that to him. Penelope? No way, they had been through too much together. And of course Luc wouldn't do something like to that to family. He cycled through all of his interactions with Gianna, Penelope, and Luc on repeat. Maybe Luc or Penelope told others. It had to have been someone else, but once again he was back at the drawing board.

They took him back to jail, a place Philippe had become too familiar with. *This again? Am I dreaming?* Deciphering reality from fiction seemed impossible, as their lines had blurred and intersected. He went through the in-take process and changed his clothes. When he stripped down in front of guards, they checked every single inch of him, including the insides of his ears, for any trace of drugs.

What felt like hours later, he was in a cold cell all by himself. He caught the words "Maximum Security" on a door as he was led to his cell. Once again, he laughed from the hilarity of it all. All this over a coq au vin recipe.

He wasn't even allowed to call anyone, just like the first time he'd been arrested. When he asked the guard about it, the guard said that since he had been deemed a flight risk, he had no opportunity for bail. It kept getting funnier and funnier. Philippe couldn't believe his string of bad, bad luck. With nothing else to do, he sat on the little metal bench in his cell, and put his head in his hands. He wanted to grab onto the bars and yell until someone freed him, but it wouldn't matter one bit.

***

It had been a long few days for Gianna, but she was finally, finally back in Paris. When she'd tried to book her flights, there had been very few options, so she had to wait a couple of days before flying out. So she'd busied herself with restaurant duties and racking her brain for ways to try to help Philippe. She had nothing, but she had no intention of giving up.

After checking back into the Four Seasons, Gianna decided to just trace some of Philippe's steps: his neighborhood, the restaurant, places he'd mentioned, the like. It was a long shot, but she decided to visit Maison de Beauchene, even though Philippe wasn't currently working there. She was hoping to talk some sense into Arnauld. If he suspected her of being in cahoots with Philippe in stealing his recipe, the best thing to do was to meet with him and explain what a ludicrous idea that was.

Even though it was spring, it was unusually chilly thanks to the looming rain and storm clouds. She put on a jacket and scarf that she'd thrown into her suitcase at the last minute and walked along the cobblestone street. She'd forgotten to pack an umbrella, and she wiped the specks of rain off of her cheeks as she made her way down the street. If it really poured, she could buy an umbrella from one of the tourist shops, but at the moment, she would rather walk than take a cab.

She was almost at the restaurant when she heard a loud crash. She looked around, along with other people on the street, trying to find where the commotion had come from. She heard another noise and realized that it was coming from the sketchy alley Philippe had led her down the night they'd snuck into the kitchen. A man on a moped had crashed into a garbage can, and a woman was hushing him. Gianna recognized her figure immediately.

Penelope! When she realized that Penelope was in the alley, she leaned against the wall at first. Then she tried to move closer, crouching and tiptoeing over. Luckily she was wearing flats, and they didn't make any noise on the cobblestones. A big garbage bin obstructed her view, so they couldn't see her as long as she ducked.

Gianna was thin but oh so tall. She wasn't sure she would make the best spy. At least she was dressed in black. She had been in a black mood when she was packing.

She strained to overhear their conversation. Penelope's voice was easily recognizable, given that Gianna had heard too much of it the last time they saw each other. She recalled the way Penelope had mocked her and cringed.

Why am I spying on Penelope? Philippe is in prison. What good will this do? Yet she kept at it. She didn't trust Penelope. It was pure instinct.

Penelope was speaking in rapid-fire French. Then Gianna swore she heard Penelope say, "Deneuve." Not willing to lose any chances, Gianna casually took out her cell phone and hit the record button. She didn't hear anything else about Philippe or anything that resembled "Deneuve," but the conversation had certainly piqued Gianna's interest. She peeked at Penelope, her phone still recording, and edged herself closer to the back of the restaurant.

Gianna was glad to be recording this. Penelope was talking to a strange man, in a dark alley, in the middle of the day about Philippe, and their conversation was clearly about some type of financial transaction.

Gianna didn't know whether her phone was actually recording their voices clearly. She raised it over the garbage can, although to raise it any higher would let them see her phone over the black garbage bags. She suppressed with all her might a need to cough. If Gianna drew attention to herself, Penelope would instantly recognize her.

"I promise you, the money is already wired," the man said. "It's safely in your account and won't be traced back to me."

He had a deep voice, which reminded Gianna of someone in the Mafia. *You've seen way too many movies.* She listened more closely, curious about their transaction. It could've been about anything, and Gianna refused to get her hopes up that it could be about Philippe.

"You swear?" Penelope said nervously. "If anything goes wrong..."

For a moment, Gianna felt sorry for her. There was true fear in Penelope's voice.

"Trust me," the man said. "Check your account balance."

Gianna didn't hear Penelope respond. She must've been checking it on her phone.

"Okay," Penelope said, a little more confidently. "It's there."

"See? You need to relax. The recipe is safe with me. Nothing will get traced back to you, me, or anyone. Do you believe me?" the guy asked.

Penelope didn't answer, or if she did, it wasn't audible.

"Do you believe me?" the guy asked again, this time with more force.

Penelope squeaked out an answer, but it wasn't a very convincing yes.

"This was your idea," he hissed. "You were the one who created this plan. Don't be backing out on me now. Me and you? We're a team."

Was it the same secret recipe that got Philippe put in the slammer? Had Penelope set Philippe up? That two-faced jerk!

Gianna knew Penelope hated her for no reason, but what had Philippe done to her? He had been there for her when everyone else abandoned her. Some friend! Gianna wanted to charge into the alley and demand some answers, but that would've been stupid. She took a deep breath and stayed still.

Besides, you can't jump to conclusions. Penelope was a chef. Their conversation could be about a dozen things. However, there was no denying the uncanny similarities. Could this be the very thing that Gianna needed to clear Philippe's name?

"I was hoping we could be a twosome in other ways," the man said.

"No way," Penelope retorted.

He laughed. "When this is all over, we can celebrate. You owe me a little fun since you created all this stress."

"Don't be disgusting," Penelope said.

Gianna shivered. The guy was a major creep on top of being a criminal. She doubled- and triple-checked her cell phone to make sure that the scene was being recorded. She couldn't take any chances. She breathed a little easier when she saw her cell phone was doing its job, but she checked it every few seconds. She decided to get a little braver and go from recording their voices to video. In order for the video to be accepted as evidence, she needed all the concrete proof she could get.

"So what's next?" Penelope asked the creep. She was out of her chef's uniform, wearing jeans and a black T-shirt. Penelope must've finished a shift.

"You tell me. You, *mademoiselle*, are the circus leader of Operation Chicken and Wine." He clucked like a chicken at her.

"Funny," she said dryly.

Penelope was tense. That was extremely evident from her rigid shoulders and crossed arms. Gianna knew that she was taking a giant risk by being so close to them, but she decided that it was worth the risk. Philippe was worth it. Besides, it was broad daylight on one of the busiest streets in Paris.

"Well, I think we need to wait until Philippe's trial is underway," Penelope said, matter-of-factly, as if she were telling the guy he needed to wait until after dinner to have dessert.

Any feelings of pity Gianna felt for Penelope quickly vanished. She gasped and could've sworn that Penelope had heard her, but Gianna couldn't stop. She kept recording, willing herself not to move a single, tiny muscle from her perch behind the Dumpster.

"Okay, then what?" the guy asked Penelope. He looked as if he was growing bored.

"So we'll wait until the trial is underway. If the police need some help believing Philippe is guilty, you can come forward and say that Philippe tried to sell you the recipe, but you turned him down."

"I thought you said we both would stay anonymous? After all, I bought the recipe from you so I could tweak it and make it even better. What if the police check into my background when I come forward? What if I come out looking like a liar?"

"Don't worry. You don't have to come forward unless it's absolutely necessary. He's already in prison, and the tabloids have basically eaten him alive. This story is too good not to believe. Nobody will suspect a thing. Seriously, it's not hard, and even if you have to come forward, you'll get some press as the noble chef."

The man said, "So I'm just supposed to lie in court? Under oath?"

"Technically. Yes, you're supposed to fib just a little teeny, tiny bit."

"I'll need some cash."

Penelope stood her ground. "No, a deal is a deal. Look, the whole goal is to make it seem like Philippe was angry with Arnauld for not allowing a menu change. Arnauld can easily testify to that."

The guy waited for her to continue.

"In an effort to get revenge, Philippe stole Arnauld's prized recipe and sold it to the competition." Penelope sounded more confident, but Gianna thought it was the stupidest plan ever.

"Fine, but if I get in trouble, you are done, do you hear me? You will be done."

"Deal," Penelope said.

They shook on it, and they looked as though they were about to leave. Gianna wanted to escape, but she was too terrified to move. What if they were coming her way?

CHAPTER EIGHTEEN

"So I guess that is it then?" the mystery man said.

Penelope nodded. "We'll talk soon. Keep an eye on the newspaper for when the trial starts. We'll meet again when it starts. I'll let you know."

"Good-bye for now, *sweetheart*." The man leered at Penelope and even lunged in for pecks on the cheeks. Luckily for Penelope, he didn't do more.

Gianna realized that the only way for the man to get out of the alley was past her or toward the backs of the buildings. Chances were he would choose to pass her. *This is bad.*

Beside the Dumpster were some cardboard boxes and a few trash cans. Without a choice, she did her best to hide behind a trash can, practically crawling in one of the dirty, wet, broken boxes. If she got caught, well... she didn't even think want to think about that. She just knew that she couldn't get caught. She told herself to count to ten and they would be gone.

The moped revved past her. Penelope must've walked in the other direction because Gianna heard her footsteps getting fainter on the cobblestone. She waited a few more minutes before deeming the coast clear, then Gianna untangled herself from her hiding spot.

"That was close," she muttered.

Should she go straight to the police station? Should she talk to Arnauld? Not wanting to add fuel to the legal fire, she decided Arnauld was the best option. She dusted herself off and walked deeper into alley. The smell of the food wafted out of the back of the restaurant. She wished she had eaten more that morning. Her stomach growled and grumbled. She knocked on the door.

A young chef popped her head out of the restaurant door and eyed Gianna suspiciously. "Can I help you?"

"I'm looking for Arnauld? He told me to stop by and use the back entrance. I'm his niece, Gabriella." *Gabriella? Niece? Where did that come from? Say as little as possible, Gianna. As little as possible!*

"I didn't know that Arnauld had a niece."

"Me either," someone else said from the kitchen.

"Hi," Gianna said brightly, keeping a big smile so as not to seem suspicious.

The chef waved her in. "Come on in. I'll point you to the office."

Gianna thought that she must've been doing something right because not only did she not get caught by that thieving Penelope, but she was able to easily get into the restaurant. She walked into the kitchen as if she owned the place, and the chef pointed her to the office. When Gianna knocked slightly, Arnauld looked up.

"Hello, Arnauld?"

"Yes, hello. How can I help you? If you're dropping off your resume, just stick in that pile over there." He pointed at a bookcase with a stack of other resumes.

"Oh, no, sir, thank you. I'm actually here in regards to the Philippe Deneuve case." She sat in the chair across from his desk.

"I'm not available for comments. Listen, sweetheart, don't get too comfortable over there."

"I'm not a reporter."

"Then what exactly do you want?" Arnauld asked impatiently.

"My name is Gianna Delano and—"

Before she could say anything else, he cut her off. "Wait a minute! Gianna Delano? You are that—that American! I should call the cops and have you arrested too, you little no good, lying thief!"

"Sir, please calm down and listen to what I have to say. I'm innocent, and Philippe is too. I have proof. Please, please will you just give me five minutes?"

"Philippe is guilty. If he were innocent, he wouldn't be in jail at this very moment. He is a no good lying thief, just like you!"

Gianna just waited politely for him to stop raging. She made herself more comfortable in his chair.

"Well?" he yelled, curious that she wasn't reacting.

"I'm waiting for you to get a grip," she said. "I have something that will change your mind."

He looked taken aback by her calm demeanor. "You aren't going to leave until I look at your so-called evidence, are you?"

Gianna silently reveled in her success.

He sat down across from her. "Who let you into my office anyway?"

"I told them I was your niece, Gabriella," she said as she pulled her cell phone out of her purse.

"I should fire them too. Oh, they're all useless. You might as well tell me what you've got."

She handed Arnauld the cell phone. "Just hit the play button and watch. It'll take you a few minutes to get through the videos, but they'll show you who is really guilty."

Arnauld pressed the play button and instantly recognized the people in the video. "I know them. Penelope. Herman!"

"Who's Herman? I know who Penelope is."

Arnauld continued watching but answered her. "He's the competition! He's a chef from another popular restaurant in Paris, but I've always been ahead of him. He's always hated me." He continued to watch the video. "I can't believe this. But Philippe? Oh my god, Philippe is truly innocent." Deep remorse and shame crossed the older man's face.

"It'll be okay, *monsieur*. Let's just get him out of there. He'll understand; Philippe is a good guy. I know his heart."

"Sweetheart, I know his heart too. He's a very good guy, which is why I feel even worse. I loved that kid, which was why I felt so betrayed. He reminds me of, well, me. He was my protégé, and I truly thought the world of him. When I found out he was leaving to work for you, and then the recipe was gone, I just... I just connected all the dots but not in the right pattern. I messed up big, didn't I, doll?"

Gianna took the old man's hand, and he looked surprised at the gesture.

"You can make this right," she said.

"You're a good one. Remind me of your name again, Gabriella?" He winked.

"Gianna," she said with a smile.

"Well, Gianna, I can see why Philippe is so fond of you. Shall we go and free your love?" He stood and gave the phone back to Gianna.

She stood as well. "I never said he was my love."

He winked again. "You didn't have to say it. I know it."

Arnauld gave her his arm, and together they walked to his car. Operation Free Philippe Deneuve had commenced.

After taking the taxi, which navigated through the busy Parisian traffic, they burst through the police station's double doors.

"Excuse me. Excuse me!" Arnauld called to anyone who would listen. "I need to speak with the investigator in charge of Philippe Deneuve's case. This is an emergency!"

The officer at the front desk typed on his keyboard. "He's not here."

"What do you mean he's not here?" Arnauld said with great dismay.

"He's at lunch. Can I leave a message?" The guard handed Arnauld a notepad and a pen.

"We'll wait. Philippe has been wrongly accused. He is innocent, and we have proof. I want to drop all the charges this instant."

"Sir, you will need to take a seat. I'll call your number when he returns." The uninterest-ed-looking guard handed Arnauld a flimsy slip of paper with the number twenty-eight on it.

"Well, this is anticlimactic." Gianna smiled.

Gianna and Arnauld had no choice except to sit and wait. And wait. And wait. And wait. The room emptied and filled back up with people just beginning their wait. Three hours later, number twenty-eight was finally, finally called.

When the investigator came out to greet Gianna and Arnauld, Arnauld told the man, "That was longest lunch ever."

The investigator ignored his comment and led them to an office. "What can I do for you? This is regarding the Philippe Deneuve case, correct?"

Gianna didn't say much. She let Arnauld do the talking and simply got lost in daydreams of what it would be like to see Philippe again. Would he kiss her the way he had in the United States? Was that just a one-night thing? No way. She thought back on his memos and the fact that he had used the L-word.

"Gianna?" Arnauld looked at her expectantly.

"Oh, sorry, what was that again?"

"The cell phone." Arnauld held out his hand, and she gave it to him. "We want all charges dropped immediately, and we want him to be freed. Please do not make him spend another second behind bars."

The investigator spent some time reviewing the files, muttering sounds but not words.

Finally, he looked up. "We can drop the theft charges, but he flew to America. That is still punishable with jail time, but it won't involve a trial. He'll meet with a judge who will sentence him, and that will be that. Are we done here?"

"Absolutely not! I want all of this dropped," Arnauld begged to little avail. "If I hadn't falsely accused him, he wouldn't be in this mess. Can't we just brush this under the rug? A hush-hush type of deal?"

"Let me call the judge. No promises. Can you wait outside for a moment?"

"Thank you, sir." Arnauld gave a satisfied nod, and he and Gianna stepped outside while the investigator called the judge.

"Do you think he's really calling him?" Gianna asked Arnauld.

"I don't know, but I sure hope so. I have some apologizing and groveling to do. It's not easy to admit you're wrong."

"You've already done the hard part. I'm sure Philippe will forgive you."

Before Arnauld could respond, the investigator came back.

"Well?" Gianna asked expectantly.

"Good news—the judge is going to turn a blind eye because Philippe's record is impeccably clean. He can be released this afternoon."

"Oh, thank God!" Gianna squealed with delight.

Arnauld clasped his hands together. "Thank you, thank you so much. Can we pick him up when he's released?"

"Yes." The investigator wrote something on a piece of paper and slid it across the table. "Here's the name and address of the prison. Be there at four thirty p.m. sharp. Good day."

With that, the investigator turned around and vanished down the long corridor. Arnauld and Gianna made their way outside to go to the jail.

***

"Deneuve, Philippe, you're free to go."

Philippe woke with a start. He had dozed off, and he couldn't tell if he was dreaming or awake.

The guard repeated himself. "Deneuve, Philippe. You're being released."

Philippe stood. He wanted to know what was happening. He exited the jail cell and followed the guard to a little room where he was given his clothes and possessions from his in-take day. He changed in front of the guard and followed him out to a little room, where he was greeted by the last two people he would had ever imagined seeing there.

When he heard that he was being released, he assumed he'd see his parents or one of his siblings—maybe even Penelope. But Arnauld and Gianna? Together? Something must've happened! He couldn't wait to hear the story, but first, he needed to do something.

At the end of the hall, he saw her, Gianna, with her hand cupping her mouth, looking as if she was about to cry. His angel.

He walked—no, ran—to Gianna, took her in his arms, dipped her backward, and kissed her as he'd never kissed a woman. There was a small round of applause from the onlookers, and time stopped. He didn't know if the kiss lasted ten seconds or ten minutes. They broke apart only when the jail guard told them to stop. Philippe helped her stand up straight.

Gianna was breathless. "Hi."

"Hi, back." Philippe looked at Arnauld, perplexed, then back at Gianna. "What are you doing here? How did you get me out? They said that all my charges have been dropped. What did you do?"

"You'll never believe this," Gianna said.

Arnauld cleared his throat. "Philippe, I'm so sorry about accusing you of theft. I was wrong."

With so many emotions swirling inside him, Philippe just looked at Arnauld. Arnauld had been a father figure to him, but his blatant mistrust had soured their relationship.

Arnauld must have seen Philippe's hesitation because he said, "I'll leave you two be for now. I'm sorry. We'll talk soon."

"I'll tell you the whole story," Gianna told Philippe, "but first, let me treat you to dinner. Anywhere you want to go, whatever you want. I just want to be with you." She looked at him shyly, yet her eyes revealed a fierce honesty that reflected his feelings for her.

"Food sounds good." He laughed, feeling happier than he had in a long time. And confused. He felt very confused. He couldn't wait to hear the story.

Over dinner, Gianna recounted everything: the eavesdropping, sneaking into the restaurant as Arnauld's niece, telling his boss, seeing the investigator.

"Penelope was the one who stole the recipe?" Philippe was in pure and total shock when he learned what shenanigans she had been pulling. How could she plot against him?

"I guess you could call her the mastermind behind all this," Gianna said. "If she had a mind at all."

"I thought of her like a sister. How could she betray me like this? Why would she want to ruin my life?"

"Not only your life but her own life," Gianna said. "I could see that she was scared, but it was as if she was beyond her own limits and couldn't stop herself."

"That's Penelope all right." He shook his head. "I just never thought she would stoop to this level. I always thought she had a lot of good in her."

"You always see the good in people. I'm sorry she let you down."

"I guess she really is that self-destructive," Philippe said. "There's nothing I can do to help her."

"Sometimes people don't want to be helped."

He looked in Gianna's beautiful eyes and nodded. She smiled and held his hands. Philippe knew with one hundred percent certainty that he wanted to work with Gianna. Most of all, he wanted to be with her; he wanted to learn everything about her.

"How long are you staying?" he asked.

"Not long. Now that we have all this sorted out, I have to go to New York. I turned down a modeling job before I left because I had the restaurant and I had to see you, but my agent called me again to convince me to take it. It's a national denim campaign, and it'll be good to add more to my nest egg."

"I see." He was disappointed, but he understood. "I thought you didn't model anymore."

"Not very often. Only when my agent comes to me with something I can't turn down. It's only for a day, then I'll go back home to work on the restaurant. You've got it all under control with the Penelope problem. I know how strong you are, especially now that you've been in jail. I just want you to know that the chef job is yours at the Parisian branch. I have a couple of spaces I'm interested in, but I need to open the L.A. restaurant first. We'll work together after we both sort out our own... situations."

Philippe beamed. "I would love nothing more than to work with you. And be with you."

CHAPTER NINETEEN

hile Philippe was out of prison and no longer considered a risk to the city of Paris or the country of France, the authorities needed him to try to catch Penelope admitting to the crime. Unfortunately, the judge and investigator had deemed Gianna's videotape inadmissible evidence. They wanted something stronger so that they could avoid a trial and just settle the matter once and for all.

On the day of the sting, Philippe woke up feeling like himself again. After all, he had slept in his own bed. He had actually eaten edible food for the past few days and wasn't being brandished as a liar, a thief, and a threat to the nation anymore.

He got dressed and put on his favorite cologne. All he knew from the investigator was that Philippe needed to go to the bench outside of some restaurant in the sixteenth arrondissement and someone would meet him there. The details were vague, but Philippe went along with it. He sat on the bench and kept checking the time. After seven minutes, he got nervous, thinking he was at the wrong spot.

Finally, a man approached him. He wore everyday jeans and a light blue dress shirt. "Philippe?"

"That's me."

"I'm Rouge. A taxi is going to show up. We'll get in, wire you, and you can go talk to Persephone."

"You mean Penelope?"

"Ah, that would be her. All right, here's the cab." As if on cue, Rouge stuck out his arm to hail the ordinary looking cab, and it stopped.

They got in, and Philippe's mind was eased when he saw that the investigator was driving. They outfitted Philippe with hidden wires. The whole situation felt like an existential, out-of-body ordeal. The investigator and Rouge coached Philippe on exactly what to say. They warned him not to stray too far off the path. Staying on topic was their biggest advice.

"All right, we'll be listening. Do not be suspicious of her. Act normal. When you hear three beeps in the ear piece, you can wrap up the conversation. Got it?" Red said.

"Three beeps, got it." Philippe saluted the crew, opened the door, and exited the cab at the entrance of Maison de Beauchene.

Maison de Beauchene looked exactly as it always had, which seemed weird. Why was it that life continued when everything in one's own life just stopped? The restaurant seemed to be running smoothly. When Philippe's life had come crashing down, everything continued on without him, as if he had never even been there. The fact that he was replaceable was a depressing but humbling thought.

When he went into the kitchen, Penelope appeared shocked to see him. He swore he also detected a hint of fear.

He held his hands out for a big hug. "Hey, Penny."

"Philippe!" she shrieked in his ear as she hugged him.

That had to be loud in the taxi. He silently chuckled at the thought.

"What are you doing here? How? Does Arnauld know you're here?" she rambled.

"Whoa, slow down. One question at a time. I'm free! Isn't that great?"

"More than great." She plastered on a smile. "That's really, really great."

Penelope poured out lie after lie. If she were a teapot, she would be empty already. She threw a potholder on the counter and pulled Philippe out of the kitchen.

"I'll be back in ten," she called to the kitchen staff.

No one uttered a word. They just continued doing their jobs.

"Sit," she instructed Philippe, choosing a restaurant table at random. "Update me. Fill me in on everything. While you talk, I'm going to work on some of these napkins." She grabbed a stack of freshly laundered black linen napkins and began folding them. "Do you want to help? For old time's sake?"

"I'm good. Okay, out of the blue, I was released. I had no idea. I thought I was doomed." As Philippe spoke, he noticed that Penelope was hanging onto his every word, frowning and looking distressed. He had been hoping that maybe it wasn't true, that maybe Penelope wasn't involved, but her strange reaction wasn't helping her case.

"Yay." She feigned excitement. "That's great."

"Yeah, so it turned out that a competing chef came forward and implicated you in the case." Of course that was a lie, but it might get Penelope to confess. Philippe didn't stray from the plan a single bit.

"No!" Penelope gasped dramatically. "Me? You—you didn't believe him, right?"

"Well—"

"I can't believe it! Which chef do you think it is? Was it your American friend? Or maybe that lady from the cat-themed restaurant that never seems to have any patrons?"

"Nope, neither of them. Do you have any thoughts? Who do you think it could be?" he asked in a calm voice.

Penelope stopped folding napkins and looked at him. "I honestly don't know."

"Seriously, Penny? No idea? Not even a hunch?" He was infuriated that she could look him directly in the eye and tell him a bold-faced lie.

She looked at him as if he were crazy. "No, I have no idea."

"I was hoping it wouldn't come to this. You know what's going on. I know you do," he said.

"Wait, are you accusing me now? Don't you dare drag me through your mess."

"Penelope." He took a deep breath. "You betrayed me. The competing chef told the police everything. Your gig is up. The joke is on you." Philippe knew her well enough to detect the true fear in her, but he could no longer be the big brother, protector type. She had ruined their friendship and their trust, and she'd tried to ruin his life. "Say something, Penelope."

"Are you trying to frame me, Philippe Deneuve? This is absurd. Arnauld was right to have you arrested. You leaving this place has been the best thing that's ever happened to him, me, the patrons, and all the employees. You're stark mad! You're a raging lunatic. They need to lock you up in a mental institution for freaks!" She was clearly panicking and trying to hurt him.

He cut her off gently but firmly. "Please stop. Please, no more. Tell me the truth. You owe me a dose of honesty. I've asked you for very little over the course of our friendship, but please, I'm begging you. Tell me the truth and cut the crap."

Penelope cried. Big, bulging tears fell down her cheeks. Philippe watched what he presumed were fake tears. The cries turned into heavy, blubbering sobs.

"Okay. Okay, I'll tell you everything," she said between hiccups.

Here it comes. His victory didn't feel as good as he'd hoped it would.

When Penelope had calmed down enough to speak in coherent sentences, she told him her version of the story from the beginning. "It started when I saw you and Gianna dining together. You looked so happy. I was so angry."

"Wait, you did this because of a silly crush?" That wasn't in the script. He shouldn't have said it.

"It was stupid," Penelope insisted. "I see it now. You've got to forgive me. You're all I have."

Not wanting to jinx his success, he said, "Just tell me what happened. I need to know."

"Fine. At first I didn't want you to leave, but then I thought that if you took Gianna's job, I'd get your job."

"You would have, correct."

"But you would still be in Paris, because that American tart wanted to open some restaurant here too. It didn't sound fair. Wherever you go, you will take my success."

"So be better," Philippe retorted.

Penelope ignored that. "So I took the recipe. I did it. I took it. I'm an awful person." She started to cry again.

Philippe didn't move. He was growing more and more uncomfortable in her presence, thinking that those three beeps would be great about now.

"I didn't mean to plant this mess on you," she said. "I meant for it to fall on Gianna. I wanted the American to go down."

"You're vindictive. Gianna is a good, honest, hardworking person. What has she ever done to you?"

"Oh, yeah right, like she's ever actually done any work. She's a pampered princess. She's fake. You're just too in love with her to see it."

He shook his head. "Just tell me what happened. Finish your story."

"Ugh, fine. So my plan was thwarted when Gianna left Paris. Everything got messed up, and then you went to jail. I had to get rid of the recipe. The coveted, prized recipe that Arnauld doesn't even need. I guess he's so old that he needed a copy in case he croaked. I didn't know what to do with it, so I had to come up with a new plan."

"Go on," he encouraged, hoping she'd go back on topic. The problem was, he actually was empathetic. That was just the type of guy he was. He didn't get mad often, and when he did, he forgave easily. But he knew he must stand firm and not give in to Penelope's antics.

Penelope refused to look at him. "I'm really ashamed, Philippe. It was a moment of weakness, and then... and then everything spiraled out of control."

"Don't you get it? These are people's lives you're destroying. Lives, careers, and even relationships. Why me, Penny? Of all the people you could hurt, why me?"

"You hurt me," she said. "I've never been good enough for you."

"I can't help who I want. You and I made the best of friends. Dating wasn't meant for us. Even you know that. You just like the idea of us." Philippe didn't want to hurt her more, even with all of the drama she had caused. He knew she was fragile. "But, Penelope, you have to know that you and I are done now, even as friends."

She grew hysterical. "You don't mean it! You would choose her, those legs, over me? Then you were never really my friend."

"That isn't true, and you know it." Philippe kept calm. "But you're poison. I cannot have that kind of poison in my life."

"I am poison," Penelope repeated, whispering.

"It's a choice you make. You don't have to be poison. You just have to choose not to be. Now, please, I need to know—why me?"

"When you were released on bail, I couldn't come clean. With the American gone, I had no choice but to frame you. When you left me the note saying you were going to America to see her, well, you made it too easy. You threw a wrench in my plans but created a golden opportunity that I couldn't pass up. Thanks for that." She jokingly sneered then seemed to realize it was an inopportune time to joke. "Sorry, bad joke."

Philippe had no words, but he mustered up the voice to tell her to continue. He clenched his fists underneath the table, hardly able to believe the words coming from her mouth. "And that's when you contacted Herman?"

"Right. I called him and told him that I had an offer he couldn't refuse, a chance to beat Arnauld for once in his life and own his coveted recipe."

Beep. Beep. Beep.

Philippe heard the three beeps in his ear piece and knew his job there was done.

CHAPTER TWENTY

*A*fter he heard the three beeps, Philippe kept to the script and wrapped up the conversation.

"Can you forgive me?" Penelope begged him.

"This is serious, Penelope. You tarnished my reputation. How can I trust you ever again? I'll try, but it'll take time. I need some space for a while." He got up and left. Outside, he walked back to the cab, where Rouge and the investigator were waiting for him.

"You did great, kid!" Rouge said, giving him a high five.

The investigator began taking the secret equipment off Philippe. "Just lay low the next few days. Don't talk to the media, and we'll handle the rest."

Red added, "Yeah, be prepared for a storm of media. Just say 'No comment' or tell them you aren't taking questions at this time. The fact that you have a famous rock star brother only makes this even more of a high-profile case."

"We'll talk soon," the investigator promised.

Lying low was exactly what Philippe did for the next three days. Aside from a trip to the supermarket, he hung out alone at home, exchanging a few emails with Gianna, and ignored all of his phone calls. He just wasn't ready to deal with the many questions from his family and friends.

On the third day of his hibernation, he woke up, turned on the television, and saw his face plastered all over the news. The whole story was revealed, and a pit formed in his stomach. Penelope now knew he'd set her up. Even though he'd had no choice, he hated that he had to do that. He watched only for a moment before changing the channel. His story was on most of the news channels. It was also in the newspapers, blogs, and all over social media.

The details in the news depicted part of the story he didn't know.

Two Days Earlier

After her unexpected conversation with Philippe, Penelope tailspun into a total frenzy. She had the mother load of all breakdowns.

She texted Herman on her disposable phone and said they needed to meet as soon as possible. He met her at a coffee shop halfway between their restaurants. In a back corner table, Penelope told him that Philippe was out of jail, his name seemed to have been cleared, and that he knew Penelope was involved.

"Darn it, Penelope," Herman whispered. "You told me that this was a foolproof plan. You promised we would be anonymous in this shenanigan."

"I know, I know! I was wrong. I messed up. We can fix this though."

"If I get blamed for this, I swear to God, Penelope—"

She interrupted him. "Just shut up so we can revise our plan. We just need to stay one step ahead of them. I have an idea."

"Yeah, I followed along with your last idea, and we can see how good that turned out for me."

"Please? We don't have any choice."

"Okay, what's your next grand scheme?" he asked mockingly.

"If you're asked anything, all you need to say is that Philippe sold you the recipe. Tell anyone who asks that you didn't know it was from Arnauld. You thought it was from Philippe. Philippe is an amazing chef—I'll give him credit for that—so it's totally plausible. Let's practice. Where did you get the recipe?"

He played along. "Philippe Deneuve sold it to me."

"Perfect!" Penelope clapped in praise. "Now, make the recipe your own with just a few minor tweaks. I took the liberty of doing that for you." She handed him a revised recipe card.

He took the card and looked over it. "Half the pearl onions? Are you crazy? Too much wine. Where is the celery? Vegetable stock instead of chicken stock, okay, that'll work. And dried thyme? Not in my kitchen!"

"You don't actually have to make it." Penelope rolled her eyes. "This just proves that you aren't stealing Arnauld's precious intellectual property. End of story! You bought a recipe from a good chef, made it your own, and you have no guilty rings in this fire. Philippe still looks guilty. He goes back in jail, and everything is back on track."

"I'll admit, this sounds like it could work."

"Good," Penelope said, satisfied.

"I'll go along with your plot, but you must promise me that I won't get in trouble."

"Look me in the eyes," she said.

He did.

Penelope said, "I promise you won't get in trouble. You aren't doing anything wrong."

"All right, we're on. This will work. This will work."

***

Like a thief in the night, the police knocked on Penelope's apartment door. "Police! Open up!"

What in the world? Penelope put on a bathrobe and opened the door.

"Penelope Solomon?" the officer asked.

"That's me. Is everything okay?" She played dumb, which wasn't hard for her.

"You're under arrest."

"Wait what? For what? You can't do this!"

"You are under arrest for conspiracy and theft of intellectual property."

One of the officers put her in handcuffs, and she kicked and screamed all the way down to the car, which made her neighbors peer out their windows at the spectacle.

They brought her to a tiny cement room for questioning. She thought that Herman had turned her in, so she had no problem throwing him under the bus. *How dare he do this to me?* The cops asked her question after question, and she had seen enough crime shows to know what was happening.

"Mademoiselle, are you sure this is the story you want to stick with? We'll give you one more chance to tell the truth," the investigator said.

"I'm telling the truth!" Penelope yelled and kicked the chair since her hands were handcuffed behind her back.

One of the officers then asked her for more information on Herman. She told them where he worked and everything she knew about him, which wasn't that much.

"Thank you. That's all for now," the officer said. "He'll be arrested next."

"Wait, what?" Penelope whipped her head around to face the officer. "What do you mean, he'll be arrested next? Isn't he the one who turned me in?"

"No, you just gave us the ammunition we need to snag him."

"What are you talking about?"

The officers exchanged glances.

When they ignored her, she yelled, "Tell me what's going on!"

"We have it all on tape. You confessed everything to Philippe Deneuve."

Penelope couldn't believe it. Philippe? She didn't know he had it in him. Her blood boiled, adrenaline rushed through her veins, and she screamed. "*Philippe!* I'm going to kill you."

"Mademoiselle, we recommend you don't say things like that. What you say can and will be used against you. I don't recommend conveying threats."

That shut her up.

***

The only phone call that Philippe answered was the one from Arnauld. Arnauld asked if Philippe could visit him at the restaurant. Cautiously, Philippe said yes.

In Arnauld's office, an awkward silence settled between them.

"Philippe, I'm sorry. I'm so sorry. This was all a giant mistake. I thought you and Gianna were out to get me. She's a lovely girl, by the way. You'll be lucky to have her in your life."

"Well—"

"I've been burned in the past," Arnauld said. "People I thought were friends betrayed me. Chefs can be such a backstabbing bunch, so competitive. I shouldn't have thought that you would be too."

"It's okay, Arnauld. Everything will be okay." He extended his hand for a handshake, as his olive branch.

The old man took it. "Would you do me the honor of coming back to your old stomping grounds? Come work for me again. I need you back. Penelope is gone, and I've got to make right by you."

Philippe thought about it for a moment, taking a sip of his tea. "I'll come back temporarily."

The old man perked up. "You will?"

"I want to work for Gianna. I've accepted her job offer of running a restaurant here in Paris, and I'm just waiting for her to finalize the purchase of a suitable building here. It's my dream job to be head chef."

"With your dream girl?" Arnauld smiled. "She's a good one, she really is."

"So I'll come back under the condition that I'll only help out until Gianna's place is ready. I will help you find and train my replacement."

"No one could ever replace you, you know that."

"Don't go getting all sappy on me now, old man," Philippe joked, always one to lighten the mood.

"So do we have ourselves a deal?" Arnauld extended his hand.

Philippe stood and took his hand. "We've got ourselves a deal."

"Welcome back. Now, go get to work." Arnauld ushered him out of his office.

Philippe was more than happy to have some normalcy back in his life. As he stepped into the familiar kitchen, a place so comfortable it was like his second home, a strange sense of calm overcame him. His life was picking up almost exactly where it had left off, but this time? This time his future looked brighter. He was in the good graces of the man who'd helped make him the chef he was, he had a dream job in the works, and maybe even a dream girl in the works as well.

Yet in the midst of all the chaos and the falling back into his old pattern, Philippe realized that a part of him was missing. Without Penelope by his side, he felt as if a limb had been severed from his body. Sure, her actions were unforgivable, and what she'd done was atrocious. But after working with her day in and day out for a couple of years, being in that kitchen without her made him lost. That emotion shocked him.

Philippe felt the buzz of his cell phone vibrating in his pocket. Arnauld had a strict no-cell phone policy. He said that if chefs were in the middle of texts, checking voicemail, or gabbing, they lost their art of cooking in the present. However, Philippe felt a sense of urgency when he didn't recognize the number, so he answered it.

"This is Philippe," he said, stepping outside. He figured the last thing he needed to do was break some more rules around Arnauld.

"Please don't hang up, Philippe. It's Penelope."

"What do you want?"

"I had my one call, and... and I didn't have anyone else to call."

"What makes you think I want to talk to you?" he coolly asked.

"I know, I know. Philippe, you have to know how sorry I am. This was all a mistake. All I ever wanted was to be a success. You know where I came from. I just wanted to rise above that and create a successful life for myself." That was her way of apologizing and asking for forgiveness.

Philippe paused in amazement. "You don't get it, do you? Penelope, you were successful. You were doing well until that wasn't enough for you. You're twenty-two and threw away an amazing career opportunity."

She sighed. "I really blew it, didn't I?"

"You did, Solomon. You really did."

"I have to go. Just know I'm sorry. All I want is your forgiveness."

CHAPTER TWENTY-ONE

*B*ack in the United States, Gianna was at Chic, Mais Oui!, putting the final touches on the menu. She needed a break, so she opened her Internet browser and checked the French newspapers.

Before she'd freed Philippe from prison, she had no idea that the Deneuve family was a target of the media. But since the recipe theft and scandal involved rock star Mathieu Deneuve's brother, the newspapers were publishing every angle of the story that they could find. One perk to that was that Gianna could stay abreast of each and every advance in the case. It seemed as though she checked the *Le Monde* site at least a hundred times a day.

When she refreshed the page, she saw that the story has been updated with a new headline: *Deneuve Family Name Cleared in Recipe Theft: Will the Real Culprit Please Stand Up?*

She read the latest update. It was all about Penelope's confession. Gianna learned how they'd wired Philippe and Penelope had confessed every last detail. The good guys won. Gianna smiled from ear to ear, so happy that Philippe was free and the real culprit was behind bars. More than anything, Gianna was thrilled that Philippe was free of such a conniving creature.

***

"Hey! I have bad news," Gianna said to Philippe on the phone. She lay in her bed and yawned as she talked, exhausted from all the work she had been putting in at Chic, Mais Oui!

Philippe groaned. "I have a feeling I'm not going to like what you're about to say."

"I have to cancel my trip. There's no way I can get everything done if I come to Paris. I work all day and all night, yet my to-do list isn't shrinking; it's growing."

"But I miss you."

"Trust me, babe, if there was any way I could pull off a superwoman act and be in two places at once, I would."

"I know. It's just that darn Atlantic Ocean. Why does it have to be so big?"

Gianna laughed then yawned again.

Gianna and Philippe hadn't seen each other since the day she'd busted him out of jail. In the time that had passed, she had chosen and purchased a location for the French Chic, Mais Oui! restaurant, but her Los Angeles restaurant opened in exactly one month. There was no way she could jet off to a different country to see the guy she missed with all of her heart. When desires and responsibilities got entangled, work usually took precedence.

"Well, just know I miss you. I wish you were here," Philippe said. Gianna yawned, and Philippe took the hint. "Listen, you sound exhausted. Go get some sleep. Dream of me. Oh, and if there's anything I can do for Chic, Mais Oui! from across the big pond, just let me know. Chef extraordinaire reporting for duty."

Gianna giggled. "Thanks and good night, sir."

The next two weeks breezed past in a giant blur, and Gianna was finally seeing her to-do list shrink and her vision coming together. Of course, she was still up to her neck in work, but she was making progress and could finally see her soft opening date as a real possibility.

The next item on her agenda was ordering inventory. Philippe had sent her a good starting checklist, but she was shocked by the number of choices there were. Everything from plates to silverware to vases to napkins and salt and pepper shakers needed to be purchased. She had an idea of what she wanted, and to do a cost comparison of three websites, she made an Excel spreadsheet full of prices, categories, and item numbers.

That took her hours upon hours, and when she got an email from Philippe, she gladly took a break to say hi.

Hey G!

All is well here in Paris. It's bizarre how normal and changed everything feels all at once. I'm back at Maison de Beauchene, and you'll never believe it, I moved. It was a totally spontaneous decision, but I found this dream apartment and I couldn't pass it up. Within a week of spotting it, I moved right in. It's a mess. I still have loads of unpacking to do! How is the restaurant business going on your end?

-P

Reading his email made Gianna ache for him. She noticed that all of their communication had gone from flirty to friendly. That probably wasn't the worst thing, since he would technically report to her, but the idea of someone else dating him made her feel rage and irrational jealousy. Maybe she was thankful for that giant ocean between them after all.

She hit the reply button.

Hey!

Good to hear from you. I'm in the middle of inventory, and wow, it is so much harder than I realized. Your check sheet has been so helpful. Tell me more about your new place. What makes it a dream apartment?

Oh, and one more thing. I'm planning on paying you a bonus for letting me use your recipes. You've earned it. Should have it in the mail to you within a few days. You have been monumental in making this place a success already. Thank you, truly, I cannot tell you how much I appreciate you.

Xoxo,

Gianna

After sending the email, she regretted adding the "xoxo" signature. Was it too flirty?

What would he think of it? Would he read too much into it?

I don't have time for this. She had a long night ahead because she refused to go home until the inventory had been ordered. Time was running out, so she ordered some Chinese food and had it delivered.

Well after midnight, she finally submitted her order and considered falling asleep right there in the restaurant. She dragged her tired, overworked body home and had never been so excited to see her bed. She didn't even change her clothes, wash her face, or turn the out bedroom light. She just collapsed into a deep, deep sleep.

The next day, after oversleeping and grabbing an apple to eat on the way to the restaurant, she felt a little bit better about her progress. Today, she had a few more interviews, which should finalize the staff. She needed two more waitstaff members and one more hostess. Gianna had some time before her first interviewee was scheduled to come in, so she pulled out her laptop, hoping for a message from Philippe. Sadly, there was nothing.

Ding!

Right as she was getting ready to close her laptop, she heard the alert that let her know she had a new message. No way! Philippe had just emailed her. She felt giddy. Every single time she saw an unopened message from him, a shiver ran down her spine. She felt like a teenager again, trying not to be that girl waiting by the phone for her crush to call. *Face it, Gianna. You are that girl.* She opened the message and read.

Gianna, you are crazy! I will absolutely not take even a cent from you for the recipes and memos. It was a gift. Gift: noun. A thing given willingly to someone without payment.

I wanted to do it, and I would do it again. I want to see you happy. I want to see you successful. You're my friend, and that's what friendship is all about.

You'll have to stop by and see the apartment when you're in Paris next. It has an amazing rooftop, and you can see the city skyline and the Eiffel Tower from there. The city lights block out the stars, but I know they're there. It's smaller than my other place, but the kitchen is more incredible. A chef's dream!

Maybe I can make you dinner when I see you? Talk soon!

-Philippe

Gianna felt silly for overanalyzing every word in the message. He had called her a friend, which meant nothing romantic. But he'd offered to make her dinner. Was that a date? Did he ask her on a date? She had no idea what was going on between them.

Not sure what to say, she vowed to respond later. She didn't want to come across as overly eager. Besides, she needed to find her questions for the interview. She asked each person applying for the same position similar questions as a starting point. While of course she was looking for people with experience, she also wanted to hire staff who fit into the vibe and atmosphere of Chic, Mais Oui! She could teach someone how to wait tables and be a hostess, but she couldn't teach someone how to be chic and charismatic. Why couldn't they all be more like Philippe?

Once all of the interviews were conducted, Gianna was officially ready to make offers. Some interviewees were duds, others had potential, and a couple were perfect. *Things are going well, Gianna.* That had become her daily mantra.

Later, Gianna focused on finalizing the placement of the furniture. She was trying to comfortably squeeze in more tables. More tables meant more diners, which meant a bigger profit. The bottom line was always at the forefront of her mind. As she worked on the placement of tables, her mind wandered to Philippe. She hadn't returned his message yet because she was confused about where she stood in his life.

She had rearranged the dining room at least half a dozen times and was satisfied with none of the options. So many restaurants in Los Angeles, or any big city, were crammed with tiny tables, and diners often bumped into the person behind them. Gianna wanted Chic, Mais Oui! to be luxurious and sleek while retaining a truly pleasant atmosphere. That meant she couldn't, under any circumstances, ignore the little details.

Her contractor, Jake, walked in as she was dragging tables around the floor. He put his hammer on the counter and took her hands off the table. "Hey, do you want some help?"

"I'm trying to figure out how to make these last two tables work with enough space."

Jake looked around for a minute. "I got it."

He told Gianna to sit put and started moving tables. She had a minor mental freak out as he ripped apart her best efforts. She kept trying to interject, but he continued telling her to hold on. As she sat and did absolutely nothing productive, her phone rang. She instantly recognized the international number on her screen.

She eagerly answered the phone. "Philippe!"

"Hi."

Gianna told him about her furniture placement debacle, and he listened. Ten minutes later, Jake had gotten the furniture placed in a way that looked like a work of art. Perfection!

"Hang on a second, Philippe." She put her hand over the receiver. "You are a genius!" she gushed as she thanked Jake.

"I'll tack it on to your next invoice," he joked.

"Funny and smart!" she teased back. She returned to her phone call. "Okay, I'm back. I was just thanking Jake, the contractor I was telling you about."

"No problem," he said.

Across the ocean, Philippe felt his heart sink. Over the past few weeks, he had been trying to figure out if the beautiful, worldly ex-super-model was interested in him or not. The way she flirted with Jake the contractor confirmed it: she had moved on.

"So we'll talk soon?" Gianna asked. "I've got to make a few calls to hire the last of my staff. I can't believe this happening."

"Good luck. Keep me posted."

Philippe kept the last few minutes of the phone call lighthearted.

He'd met Jake briefly, and even as a guy, he had to admit that the contractor was handsome. Of course it made sense that she would be with him. Philippe's breathtakingly gorgeous Gianna had a lover. She didn't want him, and it hurt.

But at least he knew where he stood. Getting ready for his own night of work, he officially let go of the hope he had been holding on to. They couldn't have made a relationship work anyway. *What was I thinking? Clearly I wasn't.* Gianna was much too busy for him. Apparently she had her hands full juggling a new restaurant and juggling too many hearts.

CHAPTER TWENTY-TWO

*A*drien Henri is in his Parisian office and has spent the past week sifting through the video audition submissions. He has literally done nothing but eat, sleep, and watch videos. Some of them have been excruciating, but he knows this is the best way to exert power over Les Slinks and keep his promise to the guys.

As the restaurant soft opening date neared, Gianna noticed her communication with Philippe becoming more and more distant. Their phone calls were fewer and further between. The tone of his emails faded from friendly banter to strictly work related. Gianna had to admit she was sad. She wondered if there was someone else in his life. He'd clearly moved on. His life was changing, and maybe she just wasn't supposed to be part of the change. Well, romantically speaking, that was.

She even wondered if that someone else could possibly be Penelope. Gianna had kept tabs on the latest developments in the case by checking in on the French newspaper every day or so, but the story wasn't nearly as publicized anymore. The media attention had died down. Philippe was definitely like the forgiving type, and Penelope was definitely the conniving type. Did they make a better fit? Could Penelope be the yin to his yang? Was she the type of woman he wanted?

If not her, there were plenty of beautiful women in Paris. Why would he want someone who didn't even live in the same country? Sure, he had kissed Gianna, but Philippe was a ladies' man. She bet he had kissed plenty of women. She wondered how many women he'd kissed since he'd kissed her.

Gianna played the treacherous *what if* game over and over. It was a slow form of torture, and she could officially relate to Penelope's jealousy. No wonder Penelope had freaked out when she realized someone was encroaching on her territory. Philippe was a great catch!

However, Gianna refused to stoop to Penelope's low level. She decided to take matters into her own hands, even if the American way was slightly more forward than the French way. Gianna pulled open her Mac and kept her message short, simple, direct, and to the point. She typed:

Philippe,

Can we have a video chat? I miss seeing your face! This afternoon, say 11 p.m. your time, after your shift at Maison de Beauchene? Let me know what you think!

-Gianna

She didn't waste another second-guessing whether she should or shouldn't send it. She needed to see and hear Philippe. She wanted to just ask him what was going on. She wanted to see his expressions, watch his eyes and his mannerisms. Nonverbal communication didn't lie.

"Just do it already, Gianna!" she whispered. She raised her finger, counted to three, and hit the enter key. "It's out there now!"

That was the thing about email. You could plan your thoughts, make them perfect, but once the message was out there, there was no way you could take it back. It was a "speak now or forever hold your peace" kind of deal.

Less than twenty minutes passed before Gianna heard the magical ding alerting her that she had new mail. She stopped examining the newest shipment of inventory, put down her checklist, and ran to her laptop. Sure enough, the message was the one she was waiting for.

Gianna,

Sure. "See" you later!

-P

Well that's the shortest message yet. She was extra glad she'd asked for a video chat because she wanted to know what his issue was. She had a couple of hours until the video conference, so she got back to work. A few of the vases were broken, so she would have to send them back, but she had only dug through three boxes thus far. Fortunately, Gianna liked organizing, so unpacking was a mindless task that helped pass the time.

Around one forty-five, she got ready for her virtual meeting with Philippe. She dug around in her purse for some makeup. In the bathroom, she touched up her blush, added mascara, and put on fresh lip balm. She ran a brush through her hair. Her eyes met the eyes of the person staring back at her from the mirror. She looked rough and tired. *There's nothing I can do about that now.* She threw her hands in the air, surrendering it all to the beauty gods.

She logged on to Skype and made a split-second decision to put her hair in a messy bun. She wore her sunglasses like a headband. She was going for the cool and casual look, a look that screamed "I'm not trying too hard." She waited. And she waited. And she waited.

Finally, at 3:06, Philippe showed up as active. She called him and waved hello, thinking that it was so good to see him. He looked much more calm and relaxed than when she'd last seen him. She could tell that things were going well for him, and she was happy but also jealous that someone else was making him happy.

"Hey!" he exclaimed.

"Isn't the Internet great?" she asked.

"It sure is. So what did you want to talk about?" He jumped straight into their conversation.

Gianna was no choice but to ask her bold question. She wanted answers, and now was her time to get them. She had the chance to actually see him and watch his expressions, so she took a deep breath before letting the words roll off her tongue. "I was just curious— are you unhappy with me for some reason?"

She fidgeted with her hands, making sure they were off-screen.

Philippe sounded as though he were unsure what she meant. "I'll say that I expected you would to be in Paris sooner. I figured you would have made more progress on the Parisian Chic, Mais Oui! by now. Remember, I'm only working at Maison de Beauchene until we get this restaurant going."

Gianna wasn't sure whether she should relax or something else was going on. He seemed agitated and curt.

All she had to go by was his answer, so she decided to reassure him. "I'm doing my best. I'm sorry I haven't made it to Paris recently. But if you're worried about the job, you should know that you're the only chef I want in my kitchen. Does that make you feel better?"

"About the job, yes."

"Does that mean there's something else going on? Come on, Philippe, please talk to me." Gianna was practically begging.

"I want to know who you want in your heart," he muttered.

"I'm sorry, I didn't catch that. Come again?" She thought she'd heard him, but she wasn't positive. She swore he'd said something about who she wanted in her heart. She had made that pretty obvious, hadn't she?

"Never mind. Just drop it." He played it off and returned to his easy-going side.

Gianna saw right through it. "No, I will not just drop it. You've been acting incredibly distant lately. Tell me what you said."

He didn't respond immediately.

Gianna watched him gather his thoughts. She was growing impatient, so she broke the silence. "I've made it very clear that I like you. I came to Paris to help free you from jail, and I'm not sure how I could be much clearer about my intentions."

Philippe still said nothing.

"Are you going to say anything at all?" Gianna demanded. He looked stumped, and she was extremely curious as to why.

"Okay, I'm just going to ask you this. Who was that guy you were talking to when we were on the phone a couple of weeks ago?"

Gianna racked her brain, trying to think of what in the world he was possibly talking about.

"Jake. You were talking with Jake the contractor," he said.

"Oh, yeah. He was helping me solve a problem I was working on. What are you getting at?" It was Gianna's turn to grow defensive. *Is this our first fight?*

"I heard you tell him that he was a genius. You laughed all flirty-like and..." He paused, probably realizing how petty and catty he sounded.

Gianna burst into laughter. "Wait. Did you think...? Jake and me?"

"So is there another guy?"

"Philippe Deneuve, you're the only man in my life."

Philippe looked embarrassed but relieved. "Really?"

"Although I do think Jake the contractor is pretty cute," she joked.

"Do I need to come out there and stake my claim?" He winked, and his tone conveyed his reassurance.

Gianna laughed. "You would need to take that up with his wife and three gorgeous kids. Seriously! Jake and his family are awesome. He's a total family man, completely devoted to his wife, and he loves his kids more than breathing. That's one of the reasons I hired him. He's the type of guy I can trust. But he isn't man I want. Loyal and trustworthy, yes. But you're those things too and more. When you aren't stealing recipes, of course."

"Oh! You just had to go there. I wish I was sitting beside you right now. Then you would really get it."

"And what does that mean, Mr. Deneuve?" Her flirting intensified.

"It means that I can think of a few things I want to do to you."

"Like what?" Gianna asked innocently.

"I'd kiss you."

"And then?"

"I would tickle you because you think you're so funny! I'd have the last laugh then."

"Philippe, I really do wish you were here. We make a good team."

"We do make a good team, Miss Delano." He looked away from the camera for a minute, looking nervous. "I think that would also make for a good relationship." He looked back at her and seemed to breathe again when he realized that she was smiling.

"What exactly are you insinuating?" Gianna played dumb, but she hoped he meant exactly what she thought.

"I don't want there to be another man in your life, Gianna. I want to be it. I want to be your guy. I don't care about the thousand miles or so that separate us. I would rather be your boyfriend and talk over email and video chat with occasional visits than not be your boyfriend at all. I know I'm asking a lot. I know there'll be challenges. I know that it would be easier if we were on the same continent, I know—"

Gianna cut him off. "Philippe?"

"Yeah?" His cheeks displayed a hint of pink from embarrassment.

"I must have been too subtle. Hear me say this loud and clear. You've already been the only man in my life for some time now. My heart is yours. I gave it to you a couple of months ago, and I don't want it back." She looked him right in the eye. "I am head over heels for you, Philippe Deneuve. Nothing you can do will change that."

"So is it official? Are you my girlfriend?"

"Yes! You're my boyfriend." She smiled. "This is the best feeling ever."

"It's settled then." Philippe gave a satisfied nod.

"Philippe?"

"Yeah?"

"You were already mine, whether you knew it or not."

Later that evening, Gianna was back at her penthouse apartment. She was surprised to see another email from Philippe, but she would never complain about that.

Hey girlfriend!

I needed to come clean about something. If we're going to do this relationship, we have to do it the right way. Trust is a huge thing with me, and so is opening up. Vulnerability isn't exactly my thing.

The other week, I went to visit Penelope in prison. I think I told you this, but I'm not sure: Penelope and I went on a couple dates a while ago. I wouldn't call it dating. We both agreed that friendship was better than dating. I know you don't like Penelope. Not many people like Penelope. What she did was awful. I refuse to make excuses for her.

But I needed to make peace with her because she has been a friend in the past. She's having a rough time in prison, and the fact is, she has no one else. I just felt like I needed to check on her. Most people would say I'm crazy. I get that. She has already made enemies within her cell unit.

She'll never learn to keep her mouth shut, I'm afraid.

She's working in the prison kitchen—not exactly the type of chef position she was aiming for. Ha! I guess what I'm trying to say is that this is me. Penelope will always be in my life, whether I want her there or not, whether I see her or not. I just needed you to know. I didn't want you to think I was hiding anything from you, because I'm not and I wasn't and I won't.

Are you mad? Is this going to be our first official boyfriend-girlfriend fight?

Love,

Your Boyfriend

This new development certainly took Gianna by surprise. She didn't understand why Philippe would ever walk to talk to Penelope or see her ever again. She also knew that behind his happy-go-lucky façade was a guy with all heart. That was who he was, and she needed to accept him at face value. *Besides, I could learn a thing or two from him about unconditional love and trust.* Philippe was such a good guy that he would forgive Penelope for almost ruining his life. That was amazing.

She pulled out a peanut butter chocolate bar, her favorite, and typed a message. It took her a few tries to get it right, but Penelope had already caused enough drama between them. There was no way their first official boyfriend-girlfriend fight would be about her. She took another bite of chocolate, mulling over her word choices.

Hi, Philippe!

Thanks for telling me about Penelope. I always appreciate the open lines of communication, but I promise that I'm not the type of girlfriend who tries to dictate your life. I have a hard enough time keeping up with myself some days! I'll be honest—I don't get your relationship with Penelope, but I can respect it. I also respect someone who goes out of their way to be kind to someone who has wronged them. I think that takes courage, and the world needs many, many more people exactly like you. Penelope is lucky to have you as a friend.

So, sorry to disappoint you, but this won't be our first official fight. It will take a lot more than you being nice to someone to make me mad!

Hugs and kisses,

Gianna

With her message sent, Gianna polished off her chocolate bar, brushed her teeth, and climbed into bed, wishing a certain someone was beside her. *That darn ocean!* Something had to give!

CHAPTER TWENTY-THREE

*A*fter their video chat session and his email about Penelope, Gianna knew there was only one thing left to do: she had to pay her boyfriend a visit. She loved that. *Her boyfriend.*

"Philippe Deneuve is my boyfriend," she said just because it made her smile.

She knew that this was the start of something new. Their emails had made them feel more like pen pals than lovers. She intended to change that. More than anything, she wanted to surprise Philippe, so she made a plan. She figured that Arnauld would be more than happy to help, and she made a quick international call.

"Arnauld? This is Gianna."

"Gianna! Lovely to hear from you! To what do I owe this pleasure?"

She told him her plan, and he was on board. She had hired a restaurant manager to take care of the L.A. restaurant while she was gone. The soft opening had gone well, and things were running more or less smoothly. All that was left to do was pack her bag and fly to see her boyfriend.

Boyfriend. Boyfriend. Boyfriend. The word wouldn't stop echoing in her mind. Of course, she didn't mind.

On the plane, Gianna knew that she was being crazy. Her schedule was more hectic than ever, but she needed to be in France. With her boyfriend. She would fly across the ocean any day just to steal a kiss from her man. For now, the flight gave her a chance to catch up on her long-lost friend, sleep. Before she knew it, she heard the flight attendant make the familiar announcement.

"Ladies and gentleman, welcome to Paris, France, and the Charles de Gaulle Airport. The time is 11:48 a.m. and the temperature is 72 degrees. On behalf of American Airlines and the entire crew, I'd like to thank you for joining us on this trip. Have a nice morning!"

She hoped she wouldn't have to hear that darn message as frequently in the future. She was ready to have her roots in one continent, even if it meant leaving her family in California. She grabbed her carry-on suitcase from the compartment above her seat and waited for the long line of people to slowly exit the aircraft. Gianna hoped that Arnauld had executed the plan precisely as they'd discussed.

About an hour before her scheduled arrival, Arnauld was supposed to tell Philippe that he was in a bind and desperately needed Philippe to pick up his sister at Charles de Gaulle. They both knew Philippe wouldn't say no. He would have a sign with a fake name on it, since Arnauld didn't actually have a sister, and he would meet Arnauld's imaginary sister at the arrivals hall.

Of course, he would actually be meeting Gianna. She hoped it would be the surprise of the century. As she made her way to the exit, her heart fluttered. She couldn't wait to wrap her arms around Philippe, run her fingers through his curls, and feel his arms around her waist. If she could run through the crowd, she would.

Finally, there he was. There was her Philippe, her boyfriend. She had exited through one door, but he was looking at another, and he hadn't seen her yet. People were swarming around like bees, and Philippe still hadn't turned her way.

Gianna was right beside him, close enough to tap his shoulder, so that was exactly what she did. At the touch on the shoulder, he turned around, and the look on his face was priceless. He looked confused, stunned, and utterly joyful.

"Gianna?"

"Philippe!" She dropped her carry-on bag and jumped into his arms, not caring who saw her public display of affection.

She wrapped her arms around his neck and hugged him. He put his arms around her waist, and everyone and everything else going on in the Charles de Gaulle airport faded away. Time stopped, and the world blurred. All that mattered was Gianna and Philippe were together.

"What are you doing here?" he whispered, unable to break the spellbinding embrace. Gianna finally pulled back, but Philippe wouldn't release her. "I swear that I'm never letting you go."

Gianna matter-of-factly retorted, "You're going to have to, because we're both very busy people."

"Oh, Gianna." He embraced her again. "What are you doing here?"

Gianna stepped backward. "I'm here to see you, of course! Are you surprised? You look surprised." She couldn't help but laugh at his expression. This was even more fun than she'd anticipated. She couldn't believe she had pulled it off.

"But how?"

Gianna told Philippe about how she'd gotten Arnauld on board with her plan.

"There's no sister coming?"

Gianna laughed. "Not that I know of!"

"I didn't think he had a sister, but I just can't believe you're here! Let's get out of here." Like a perfect gentleman, he took her carry-on and grabbed her hand. "You have interesting timing, missy. After I dropped off Arnauld's nonexistent sister, I was going to meet up with some of my family. Is it too soon for you to meet them? I'll warn you, they're awesome but loud and crazy."

"Are you kidding? I'd love nothing more than to meet than your family!"

Philippe's heart swelled. Could he love her any more? He almost blurted that out.

He opened a taxi door for her. He hoped that his siblings would like her, although he had no doubt that they would. Who wouldn't like Gianna? Well, besides Penelope. "This is crazy. My worlds are colliding."

"So where are we going?" Gianna asked as the taxi pulled away.

"Actually, back to my place." He gave the driver his address. "A few of my brothers and sisters are coming over for a little housewarming. It's casual, nothing fancy, but they want to see my new place."

"I can't wait to see it," Gianna said.

Philippe called one of his brothers on the way and let him know he was coming and that he had a very special guest with him.

"Do they know anything about me?" Gianna asked.

"They only know a little bit. I don't bring a lot of girls into my family life."

"So this means I'm extra special, right?" She winked.

"You know it!" He squeezed her hand. He couldn't keep his hands off of her, but he stayed a gentleman.

When they got to his house, Gianna exclaimed, "You live here? This building is incredible."

"Thanks," Philippe said. "Come on, you ready?"

"Yup!"

They were actually the last ones to arrive. His brothers and a sister were waiting in the living room.

"Hey, guys," Philippe said. "Welcome to Casa Deneuve. This is Gianna Delano. Gianna, this is Mathieu, who you've met already. This is Luc, Madeleine, and Xavier."

"It's nice to meet you." If Gianna was shy, she was feigning it.

Luc raised his eyebrows at Philippe as if to say, "Good going."

Philippe, always the impeccable host, excused himself to get the food. He returned to living room with a few trays of finger sandwiches, brownies, a fruit and vegetable assortment, and sparkling waters garnished with lemons and limes.

"This is why we hang out at Philippe's house," Xavier told Gianna as he picked up a sandwich triangle. "Possibly the only reason."

"He can cook, that's for sure." Gianna laughed.

"Don't make me blush, guys," Philippe joked back.

They filled their plates and ate, catching up on the latest Deneuve family gossip. Gianna had only one brother, so all of this was a new world for her, but she loved being a part of it. Philippe's siblings were all so nice and funny too. Xavier and Mathieu were more outgoing, cracking jokes. Luc was a bit more reserved, which balanced them out. He was probably the voice of reason in the family. Madeleine was so smart that Gianna would be intimidated if she wasn't so warm and friendly as well.

Gianna sat back and observed them, realizing that the Deneuve family was a rare gem. They all seemed so close, finishing each other's sentences and seeming so comfortable and happy in each other's company. It made her wish that she had siblings. She had cousins, but they didn't live in the same state, so it wasn't the same at all.

Once the gossip had been dished out, Madeline said that they needed to teach Gianna the game.

"Oh no!" Philippe said. "Not the game."

Gianna just laughed. "I'm up for anything."

"Famous last words. Don't agree to everything we suggest," Mathieu advised.

But it was too late. Madeline had already gone to the kitchen, rummaged through Philippe's drawers, and returned with a deck of cards and a handful of spoons. "The game is called, I think, Spoons in English. It's a Deneuve family favorite, but I have to warn you, we get vicious playing it. There's no lack of competition."

"I love this game," Gianna exclaimed. "The card game, right?"

"No way! You know it?" Philippe looked impressed.

"Of course! I played it in college all the time."

"It's settled, Philippe. This girl is officially the best woman you have ever brought home," Xavier said.

"Yep, you've got to keep her!" Madeleine said.

Mathieu piped up. "Yeah, don't mess it up."

"Trust me, I'll bring her around as long as she'll have me." He beamed at his girlfriend.

Gianna beamed back at him.

"Wow, you two have it bad," Luc said.

Gianna nodded ever so slightly. That more than true. They played, and Gianna chatted with his siblings. After a few hours of being surrounded by Philippe's warm and loving family, Gianna could see herself living a less busy life, slowing down to be with Philippe. Her heart wanted it, and her body wanted him. Every ounce of her soul wanted a life with Philippe. She wanted to be with Philippe every single day, sharing every single boring moment of life. She was willing to do anything to make that a possibility.

She was nervous about approaching the subject, but after her potential future brothers- and sister-in-law left Philippe's house and it was just the two of them, she decided to bring up the subject. He brought her tea, sat beside her on the couch, and rubbed her leg. After a long day, that moment of relaxation was exactly what she wanted and needed.

Slightly cautiously, Gianna said, "I was thinking about extending my holiday here, with you."

"Really? I would love that."

"Yeah, the restaurant is up and running and doing well. The chef is perfect. I think that it's high time that I focused on something more important."

"What would that be?" he said.

"Love," she said quietly.

Philippe looked at her and seemed happy to hear her mention the L-word. "Did you just say what I think you did?"

Gianna nodded with only the slightest movement.

"Look at me, Gianna." He sat up beside her and took her hands. "I love you. I love you with my entire heart. You're everything: beautiful, humble, smart, and funny. You make me come alive. I love you, Gianna Delano!"

Gianna gave him a short, soft kiss. "I love you, Philippe. I've loved you since that first day you tried to cook for me. When things went horribly wrong, you tried to cook for me again at Maison de Beauchene."

"And we all know how that went." He laughed.

"Horribly?"

"Yup. But we're here now, and I get a lifetime to make it up to you."

They snuggled for a moment. She pressed her ear against his chest and listened to his heartbeat. After a few moments of relaxation, Gianna yawned, her exhaustion settling in.

"Instead of going to your hotel, stay here," he said. "You can sleep in the guest room. I like knowing you're close by."

"Okay." Gianna said, settling on the couch instead. It was just so cozy.

Philippe took her empty tea mug and brought her a blanket. "Good night, beautiful." He kissed her cheek.

"Philippe?"

"Yes?" He turned around right before he turned out the light.

"I love you."

"Oh, Gianna, I love you. See you in the morning."

CHAPTER TWENTY-FOUR

*A*s he rides in the backseat of a taxi, Mathieu starts to realize the magnitude of this situation. He becomes angrier with each second that ticks by. How could Adrien do this? What about Marcel, Olivier, and Guillaume? How could they just go along with this?

What a year it had been! Gianna and Philippe had met for the first time exactly one year ago. Now their lives were intertwined and, in some ways, completely different.

Gianna was in Paris and had just read the latest magazine review of her Chic, Mais Oui! restaurant. Both her Los Angeles and Paris locations were thriving.

The latest review out of LA read: *Chic, Mais Oui! adds a new level of style and sophistication to the LA foodie scene. You've got to try the scallops, take their suggestions on wine pairings, and the risotto should not be skipped. Exquisite, exceptional food. Not a single detailed is missed in ambiance, food presentation, or quality. This is a must-try place. You will become repeat customers, like me!*

She rummaged around the kitchen drawers until she found a pair of scissors. She cut out the review and put it with in a scrapbook with the others. Most of them were rave reviews, but of course, a couple of reviews were just okay. Either way, they were a part of the Chic Mais Oui!'s tapestry, and she weaved in the good and the bad.

As Gianna flipped through the scrapbook, she couldn't help but get lost in nostalgia, reminiscing about everything that had happened. She felt as if she'd woken up in someone else's life, in a new country with a new last name.

Some days, Gianna missed California and the United States, but her heart was in Paris. Over the last twelve months, Gianna had continued flying between continents for a little while. She'd needed to be present at both Chic, Mais Oui! locations, especially starting out. There were press interviews, details to attend to, but

Gianna only felt complete when she was with Philippe.

Philippe had told her that he knew she was his bride-to-be. He knew she was tired of the flights, and she knew that he wanted to stay in Paris with his family. Besides, she loved Paris and needed Philippe to be in control at the Paris restaurant. They'd hinted at marriage, but they weren't in a rush. They were just surfing the wave of success and enjoying the ride of the relationship.

When Philippe decided to take the plunge, he had found himself at a jewelry store near Chic, Mais Oui! He went in every single day for a week, looking at rings and chatting with the manager, who was extremely kind and patient. But Philippe kept coming back to one ring: a bead-set princess-cut platinum ring. He had no idea what type of ring Gianna liked, but that one called to him.

So after a week of visits with the ring, he handed over his credit card and left with a tiny black velvet box. He had purchased the ring, but he was terrified to actually give it to her. What if it was too soon? They had only been an official couple for a few months at that point. All he knew was that he couldn't live without her. He needed Gianna, and he was pretty positive she felt the same way about him.

On her next trip to visit him, they sat on the balcony, watching the Parisian skyline. Gianna was under a blanket and telling him about when she used to go camping with her family during the summers. Her favorite part had been eating s'mores.

Philippe had kept the ring box in his pants pocket, with no real plan or idea as to how to propose. He wanted it to be spontaneous. But sitting on the balcony, he finally mustered up the courage. He told her he was going to give her a dessert that would make her forget all about s'mores.

When he came back with a plate, he had it covered. "Can you guess what it is?"

"Umm, tiramasu?" she guessed. She took off the cover and gasped when she saw the ring. "Philippe!"

He had never been so nervous. He got down on one knee and asked her to be his forever partner in life. Of course, Gianna said yes!

After the proposal, things moved quickly. They didn't want to wait for a drawn-out courtship, engagement, or fancy ceremony. However, it was important to Gianna to get married in America, since her parents weren't keen on flying. So the Deneuve family took on America and watched Philippe and Gianna get married in a California vineyard. The wedding was small, perfect, and full of good food! It couldn't have been more perfect—well, except for the light tremble of an earthquake. Right as the ceremony officiant said, "You may now kiss the bride," a small tremor could be felt by all in attendance. What could they say? Philippe and Gianna's love could literally move the earth.

Back in the US, she quickly sold her penthouse apartment. Less than two weeks later, her address had changed to a Parisian one. Gianna moved in with Philippe, and they both thought life was pretty extraordinary, even on the boring, mundane days. Philippe ran a tight kitchen at Chic, Mais Oui! in Paris. Working as the head chef was his dream job. He had control over the menu, the opportunity to be creative, and his staff loved him. He pushed them to be creative and test their own skills. More than anything, he loved getting to spend practically every waking hour with his stunning wife, Mrs. Gianna Deneuve.

After she put her scrapbook away, Gianna burst into their restaurant's kitchen and put her arms around Philippe, who was at the stove. She whispered in his ear, trying to lure him away from the stove for just a few moments.

"I can't right now, lady!" He pointed at the vegetables being sautéed in coconut oil.

"Burned vegetables means we can't serve them, which means wasted food, which means less profit."

"Ugh, I hate it when you're right." She pouted.

"The night is young, babe!" He kissed her cheek.

Of course he was tempted. What guy wouldn't be tempted by her sultry ways? Philippe thought Gianna was gorgeous when she woke up without a trace of makeup. He thought she was beautiful when she was hacking up gunk when she was battling the flu. He thought she was beautiful when she tried and when she was in sweatpants and an old ratty T-shirt. What made Gianna beautiful wasn't just her looks. He was smitten because of her personality, her sincerity, and her conviction. She was strong, independent, and stunning. He was still waiting to find a flaw. So far, the only thing he had come up with was that she didn't clean the toothpaste out of the bathroom sink after she brushed her teeth. What could he say? He was a lucky guy indeed.

Okay, and sometimes she drove him crazy, as she was doing right then. He pulled her hands off of his waist and kissed her cheeks.

"Gianna..." he said in his best warning voice.

"I know, I know!" she teased.

No one else in the universe had the same effect on her. She had dated plenty, but true love waited, and she would have waited a thousand years more for just one day with her husband. She'd always thought she would have a couple of kiddos and a vacation home by now. Being a restaurant owner, Philippe's wife, and a new Parisian was a hand of cards she'd never imagined being dealt. But they were in front of her, and she never wanted to play another round. She had already won.

Tonight was a big night. All of Philippe's family was coming for dinner. Of course, that meant Philippe wanted to show off a little bit.

He loved his family gatherings even more now that Gianna was officially one of them. The feeling of having all of his favorite people in one place was insurmountable. Gianna, his siblings, and his parents together was a slice of heaven on Earth.

Determined to pull him away for just a second, Gianna said, "Well, I'm your boss, and I really need to pull you away for a second. There is something I need to discuss with you."

Looking skeptical, he rolled his eyes. Philippe asked his sous-chef to take care of the pan and held up five fingers. In her office, Gianna closed the door.

"What could possibly be so important that you had to drag me away from the kitchen?"

Gianna could tell he was slightly annoyed even though he was trying hard to keep up a façade of being cool, calm, and collected.

"This has nothing to do with Chic, Mais Oui!, but I think there's a tiny chance that there might be a..."

"A what?" Philippe was obviously clueless about what Gianna was hinting at.

"A mini-Philippe or mini-Gianna on the way." *There!* She'd said it. Philippe didn't say anything for a minute, and Gianna watched him process the news.

"Wait, are you saying what I think you're saying? Are you...? Are we...?"

Gianna couldn't tell if he was excited or nervous or mad. "My period is late. That never happens. I'm going to take a pregnancy test in the morning, but I couldn't wait another second. I had to tell you."

Philippe was silent again.

Gianna hated when he did that. "Say something!" She started to tear up and panicked that he didn't think this was a good thing.

"Gianna, are you kidding me? You aren't messing with me right now, are you?"

She shook her head.

"Sweetheart, this is incredible! I'm shocked, but this is the best news ever! I hope our kid looks just like you and is exactly like you. What should we name the baby?"

She beamed. "Slow down. Wait until I know for sure before you start getting anything monogrammed. Don't say anything tonight. I don't want to announce our speculation, if that is okay with you."

"Sounds good to me. I can't wait to know what's going on, with the baby and with the big announcement."

Someone knocked on the door.

"Come in!" Gianna called.

One of the kitchen staffers came in. "I'm sorry to bother you, but can you come back to the kitchen? The chicken needs your help. It looks like we're short a few pounds."

"I'll be there in just a second," Philippe said. The girl closed the door, and Philippe turned back toward Gianna. "All right. I've got to get back to work. I wouldn't want to get in trouble with the boss." He winked.

"So you are happy?" She asked, needing confirmation.

"This is the best news ever! I'm more than happy." He kissed her forehead. "Let me know when the family starts arriving."

"Will do."

Once Philippe left, Gianna went out to the front of the restaurant. She helped the hostesses, ran food between the kitchen and the tables, and checked on guests in the dining room. So far it had been a flawless night at Chic, Mais Oui!

A large table was reserved for the Deneuve family, and slowly, seat by seat, it filled up with her mother-in-law, father-in-law, and all Philippe's brothers and sisters. She hated calling them in-laws, because to her, they were just family. They all greeted her warmly and gave her American-style hugs.

"Okay, I'm going to grab Philippe," she announced and went back to the kitchen. She found Philippe and whispered, "They're all here, *papa*."

Philippe couldn't stop grinning. Keeping their secret would be tough. Together, they walked to the dining room and took the last two seats at the table.

Always the teaser, Philippe sat and said, "Okay, I'm here. Let the party begin."

Chloe Emile

ABOUT THE AUTHOR

Chloe Emile writes sweet, clean romance, whether it's contemporary or historical. She can usually be found working on her next novel, eating takeout with her husband, or watching rom-coms.

Visit her website for the latest updates.

www.ChloeEmile.com

www.ingramcontent.com/pod-product-compliance
Lightning Source LLC
Chambersburg PA
CBHW052039240626

47153CB00006B/2156